Before Brezhnev Died

Iulian Ciocan

BEFORE BREZHNEV DIED

Translated from the Romanian by Alistair Ian Blyth

DALKEY ARCHIVE PRESS
McLean, IL / Dublin

Library of Congress Control Number: 2019953493

Dalkey Archive Press
McLean, IL / Dublin

Co-funded by the Creative Europe Programme
of the European Union

Printed on permanent/durable acid-free paper.
www.dalkeyarchive.com

To my parents, alongside whom I lived this "novel"
for an eternity

Contents

To Georges Perec, who, unfortunately, is no longer alive

Other Things

WITH A PANG of the heart, Olga Leonovna decided to sell the family home she had inherited after the death of her grandparents. After exhausting negotiations, Vladimir Vladimirovich had borrowed a fabulous sum of money from acquaintances, and in the summer of 1967, Iulian's parents obtained a poky apartment in a building that had just been constructed in the Ryshkanovka district. They had paid half the price of the apartment, with the remaining half to be paid off over the course of ten years, which required them to make Sisyphean efforts, but despite that, they were happy. They were not Party members, public functionaries, Writers of the People, or qualified engineers from Novosibirsk or Omsk for them to have any prospects of ever receiving a free apartment. They knew that by force of circumstances they could succeed only by relying on their own perseverance.

In the first few months, during which they slept on a decrepit folding bed in the middle of an empty room thick with the smell of whitewash, it even seemed to them that the apartment was spacious. Doubt as to that began to gnaw away at them on the day when they moved in all their belongings. With a surface area of forty-one square metres, as they had verified countless times, their apartment consisted of a tiny vestibule, a minuscule kitchen, a medium-sized bedroom, an all-purpose room—sitting room, guestroom—and a balcony which over the years was to become a moldy extension of the bookcase. Gradually, the refrigerator, the vacuum-tube television, the beds, the chairs, the armchairs, the cupboards, the bedside tables and the sideboard—most of them purchased on credit—considerably limited their free space, confining their movements. The truth that they did not wish to recognize at first—that the two-room apartment was the most they could achieve, that they would never manage to move into one that was genuinely spacious—irremediably made them captives of a pointless, wearying ritual: At least once every three months, they moved the furniture, trying to hit upon the perfect arrangement that would allow them to salvage two or three extra square metres of essential living space. They debated at great length about whether or not they should put the wardrobe where the bed was and move the bed to where the bedside table was, on which perched the vacuum-tube television set with its abominable picture. Their words would be accompanied by vigorous gesticulation and sometimes they even quarreled. They demolished a thin wall, moved the refrigerator into the vestibule, attempted to convert the balcony into a small room, installing an extra radiator. At the end of it all, they came to the bitter conclusion that the forty-one square metres had not been enlarged a single jot. They had to buy furniture, it was an undiminished requirement, naturally, but at the end of it all they risked ending up in a suffocating birdcage.

The lack of space became tyrannical after Aunt Sanya moved in with them. Recently retired, she had been left homeless after the death of her husband, with whom she had not had children. Her deceased husband's relatives had evicted her, vociferating about how she was supposedly trying to obtain other people's property by fraudulent means. Aunt Sanya had left, since she wasn't a fraudster and had genuinely loved her husband. Life's misfortunes had not embittered her, they had not made her lose heart, they had not, surprisingly, shattered her peace of mind. The only thing she brought with her when she arrived was an icon, much to the exasperation of young Iulian the pioneer. The lad tried to oppose it, he invoked the school textbooks that vilified religion, with tears and

heavy sighs he said that he refused to eat unless that
tool of the international bourgeoisie were thrown in
the trashcan. "Shut it, snot-nose! It's not your house
for you to decide!" roared his father, brandishing his
fist and ordering him to do his homework, which is
to say, to read the very textbooks that fueled the lad's
atheism. Feeling guilty at intruding on them, Aunt
Sanya undertook to pay their electricity, gas and
telephone bills out of her pension. Iulian's mother
and father shrugged, but their situation demanded
they accept her help. Moreover, Aunt Sanya—with
whom Iulian now shared the smaller room—set about
scouring the city's parks and the young forest between
Ryshkanovka and the Old Post Office (which the
post-communist period was to transform into an
unauthorized rubbish dump and junkie stronghold)
to collect the empty bottles that sprouted there like
mushroom after the rain. Often till dusk, she assiduously collected milk bottles, mineral water bottles, and, of course, vodka and wine bottles, whose
number was overwhelming. She knew all the street
sweepers. She earned around ten rubles a week from
this occupation, money she spent on buying Iulian
ice cream with glacé fruit, Snezhok candies, corn-
flakes, and Buratino lemonade. Sometimes, Iulian's
mother would suggest that eggplants and tomatoes
were healthier for the boy than candies. Sometimes,

his father would furtively urge Aunt Sanya to buy vodka or brandy. They would usually tipple when Iulian's mother was out at the Strǎșeni market selling the mohair sweaters she knitted. Bent double with heavy shopping bags, Iulian's mother returned home late and took them to task. They began to quarrel. Iulian's father yelled that he toiled like a slave at the factory and that his wife nagged him for every little thing. Aunt Sanya would say that Iulian's father wasn't to blame because she had been the one who wanted to treat her nephew-in-law to a drink. Drained by insomnia, Iulian harbored doubts as to the blamelessness of his father, whose eyes cast daggers at him. At night, the two-room apartment filled with the hellish snoring of Iulian's father and Aunt Sanya's mumbling in her sleep, which made even more unbearable the thoughts of death that already tormented the introspective pioneer. Iulian had become taciturn and pensive from the day when his mother left hospital and returned home without his long-awaited little brother. He understood everything as soon as he saw her: haggard and downcast, she spoke haltingly, like a stranger.

"I've weighed things up with your dad . . . it would be hard for us if you had a little brother *right now*, but you'll have one in a couple of years . . ." said his mother, wringing his hands.

The words seared his heart.

The manner in which his mother had uttered them convinced him that he would *never* have a brother or sister, that he would be alone his whole life. One sleepless night, an even more terrifying thought budded in his mind: it followed that he himself would not have existed had he not been born before the sibling doomed to perish. He was alive only because he had been born first. And the fact that he had been born first was down to chance and could not have been planned even by the General Secretary of the Communist Party of the Soviet Union himself. Consequently, there existed a reality independent of our will, which blatantly undermined any faith in a predictable, radiant future.

Day and night, they thought about how to make money. They noted with bewilderment that Vera Nikanorovna the pharmacist, a poor widow from the next building, had got herself a washing machine. They couldn't afford to buy wallpaper, let alone a washing machine. His mother's hands were constantly chafed, callused. True, they had managed to procure a vacuum cleaner, which wailed like a siren every Sunday, and, over the course of a decade, two Persian rugs, a television set that needed repairing year after year, a refrigerator, a record player, three crystal vases, a gas cooker, and a couch. They tightened their belts and laid parquet flooring. They tiled the poky kitchen, but not the bathroom, since the money had run out. The purchase of every item was a small victory in a war whose duration was equal to that of a human lifetime.

WRITER A.L.: *The village Baurci has three schools, nurseries, kindergartens, a hospital, a maternity ward, a store selling mass-produced goods, and a bookshop. Last year, the local collective farm workers bought 180 refrigerators. 108 people have put their names down on the waiting list for cars. Not to mention the new, beautiful, spacious houses that they are building themselves. "The state helps us a lot"—I have heard these words dozens of times, I have heard them spoken with respect, confidence and gratitude.*

To worker Vladimir Vladimirovich, three things were sacrosanct: parquet, tools, documents. Every Sunday, he would wake up very early in the morning and on his hands and knees he would wax the parquet until the sweat streamed off him. It had become a custom that consumed the last vestiges of his energy. The apartment had become a skating rink. Aunt Sanya would lose her balance and fall over, emitting a piercing screech. "What's got into you?" Iulian's father would yell at her. He would thunder and fulminate if so much as a drop of water spilled on the parquet.

He would constantly warn Iulian that the costly parquet could not tolerate wetness. His tools, worth a
small fortune, he kept crammed in a little cupboard
on the balcony. Nobody was allowed to open the cupboard, inside which rusted his welding gun, plastering
spatula, screwdrivers, screws, nails, pliers, round and
triangular files, nuts, bolts, ball bearings, saws, ham-
mers, ferrules, a few rasps, and slide rules. In the middle of that heap of scrap metal nestled a jar of mastic
and another of bronze dust. Since Iulian's father knew
the contents of the cupboard by heart, it was risky
to remove even a couple of nails. But nothing could
compete with the family documents. These had to be
guarded like the eyes in your head. They had to be
kept in a safe place, inaccessible to any visitor.

"Without your identity card, you're nothing!"
explained his father. "Without your identity card,
nobody will take any notice of you! Understand me?"

Iulian did not understand.

The passage of the years—each perfectly resem-
bling the next—reinforced their suspicion that things
were going worse and worse. Each New Year found
them wearier, older, more obsessed with saving
every kopeck. They toiled from inertia, bent double
by the all-pervading pointlessness. No matter how
hard they strained, their wages remained the same.
Only a miracle could rebuild from its foundations

that dreary life of serial automatism. Even the housing block gave signs of premature exhaustion. The bitumen roof had fissured and—since they lived on the top floor—rainwater trickled down the walls of the balcony. Previously ignored, the weather forecast was now meaningful, listened to every morning. Torrential rain was a cause for anxiety. They would beg Aunt Sanya not to go out bottle-collecting that day, to stay at home to do battle with the puddles that might flood the balcony. Aunt Sanya would prepare for battle by taking a basin onto the balcony, along with a number of jars and a huge rag that had once been a bathrobe. Iulian's father would go to the chairman of local residential buildings committee and beg him in the name of all that was holy to repair the roof. With slight irritation, the chairman would promise that the issue would be addressed. A few apathetic workers would climb up onto the roof and idle the day away, yelling at each other all the while. The balcony would continue to be flooded. In order to beat the rainwater, the top-floor tenants roofed their balconies with slate. The water was reduced, but the mold was ineradicable. The roof required thoroughgoing repairs. They asked for the assistance of the lower-floor tenants, who said that they couldn't care less about the roof. Their problem was blocked toilets.

WRITER G.M.: *Each looks after the wellbeing of everybody else and everybody looks after the wellbeing of each. Was there ever such a state in the history of the world? Never! The wise men of old barely dreamed of such a thing.*

Little by little, the inconveniences multiplied: in summer the walls peeled and flaked; the wall sockets and light switches frequently gave off sparks; the rumbling refrigerator fell silent after a short circuit; the rusting pipes dripped; the bathtub yellowed as fast as the eye could see, although it was frenziedly scrubbed; cockroaches and ants did fierce battle in the kitchen, with the cockroaches gaining the upper hand during the cold months, as insecticides were ineffectual; moths—Iulian's mother's mortal enemy—methodically gnawed their clothes and the Persian rugs; somebody stole their mailbox; the furniture filled with scratches, driving Iulian's father insane, and Iulian was held guilty and threatened. Paying the loans was onerous. They were mired in debts. And worse still, they had to eat every day. Often, his father would board the bus, crammed with peasants, the air thick with stench, that went to the village of his Aunt Talyusya, two hundred kilometres from Kishinev. He would come back with potatoes, garlic, apricot and raspberry jam, walnuts, a hen or a turkey. Iulian was very fond of Aunt Talyusya's raspberry jam.

Despite all this, one certainty helped them elude the toils of despair: There were people even more unfortunate: families who lived in the twelve-square-metre rooms of hostels where it stank of borsht and urine; parents whose children had died in accidents; lonely invalids. They always thought sorrowfully of the Boaghes, whose children had been killed in a devastating fire and who had lost everything they had. The grief-stricken wife had tried to commit suicide and ended up in an insane asylum, and her husband had drunk himself senseless. As for Iulian, he was terrified by the official news bulletins about the harsh life of the working class and black people in capitalist countries.

The nicest evenings were when his mother made them cheese and pumpkin pie, poured them rosehip tea from a brightly painted Chinese thermos flask that reawakened nostalgia for Sino-Soviet fraternal relations, and told him stories about times past. Hanging on her every word, the lad with the elongated head discovered marvelous things. Flushed, excited, suddenly transfigured, his mother would evoke a wonderful time when his father was handsome, gallant, full of energy, when he didn't drink, when he dressed with taste and sometimes took her to the Restaurant Doina or even the theatre. His father would smile and give him a wink.

"You're lucky, Olga . . ." Aunt Sanya would say, then sigh heavily, remembering her late husband.

Sometimes, his mother would talk about the years before the war: "We used to live in clover, didn't we, Sanya? Our parents had a plot of land near the Dniester, we could ride in the carriage to the fair, Mother, God rest her soul, would buy us all kinds of clothes, she used to feed us walnuts."

Iulian's eyes would bulge in indignation: "How could that be? You were occupied by the Romanians at the time!"

"What did that have to do with it? They were good times . . ." his mother would say, dreamily, rashly.

"Maybe for you!" His father would grow taciturn and put an end to the reminiscences. He would turn his gaze to Iulian: "Now you get to bed!"

WRITER A.B.: *Would they ever have been able to dream, those starving, naked children of the late 1930s, tending wretched goats along strips of waste ground and the roads of a Bessarabia groaning under the boyar occupation, that a day would come and they would become people of importance, leading figures in this flourishing, agro-industrial*

Soviet Socialist Republic? Yes, they would have been able to dream; the dream is the final redoubt to fall inside a man, but only Soviet Power helped them see their dream come true.

One day, his mother came back from the nursery school more radiant than she had ever been before. The father of a child in her group had a cousin who worked at the apparatchiks' store and he had given her two tins of caviar and a jar of olives. Thitherto they had not known that anybody who had access to the apparatchiks' store, although naturally they knew that somewhere far away that realm of opulence existed, inaccessible to mere mortals. Their hopes were now reborn. They no longer queued for Doktorskaya sausages. They bought some jeans, an East-German jacket and a pair of Polish shoes for Iulian at a reasonable price. But other than that, everything was the same as before. The wearying travail seemed to have no end. In the future there yawned liked an abyss the post-communist transition period that would lead them to sell their apartment and take refuge in the countryside. Many of their old things—taken out by the removal men urged to haste by the new owner—were to be thrown in the garbage or given away to neighbors, with the feeling that they were relinquishing a part of their very being.

A Rotten Tomato

LOBBED WITH SHARPSHOOTING precision from the fifth floor of the apartment block, the rotten tomato exploded right on top of Polikarp Feofanovich's gleaming baldpate. For an instant, the recently pensioned war veteran was gripped by a crippling panic, which straight away transformed into embarrassment and amazement at the reeking viscosity trickling down his face and neck. He wanted the earth to swallow him up. He felt that all eyes were fixed upon him. From somewhere above, a neighing laugh could be heard. With trembling hand, he extracted a crumpled handkerchief from his trouser pocket, glancing fearfully around him. Although it was the middle of the day, the courtyard was deserted. He sighed in relief. He lifted his gaze and scrutinized the upper storeys of the apartment block. The longish face of

a child was peeking from behind the concrete balus-
trade of the balcony that perched under the eaves of
the roof, crammed with all kinds of useless objects.

All of a sudden, he recalled how Veniamin
Nikanorovich, the defender of Stalingrad, the friend
with whom he used to play dominos and go fishing
for carp at Gidigich, sometimes complained that he
had been "bombarded" with rotten eggs and tomatoes
in broad daylight. Polikarp Feofanovich now realized
that he had not taken seriously a matter that was far
from being innocuous. He had serenely ignored an
impiety which, in the normal course of affairs, ought
to have given him cause for thought: children—who
must also be pioneers or Komsomol members—were
making a mockery of the veterans of the Soviet Army.
Prey to troubling pangs of conscience, he also remembered another detail: Veniamin Nikanorovich always
told him of these incidents in a hushed voice, avoid-
ing his eyes. What is more, Polikarp Feofanovich's
opinion that they were just childish pranks grated
on Veniamin Nikanorovich's nerves. Once, when the
recently pensioned veteran was unable to contain his
laughter on hearing the whispered words evoking the
comical drama of his friend caught in a rain of rotten
eggs, the defender of Stalingrad had turned his back
on him and refused to speak to him for days on end.

Set to thinking, Polikarp Feofanovich felt an

imperious need to urinate. His bladder was about
to burst, transmitting him desperate S.O.S. signals.
He looked around him, hurriedly went over to the
stunted bushes in front of the grey apartment block,
squatted, removed his shriveled member, and pissed
interminably, intermittently, straining and turning
red in the face. A housewife, her back bowed by the
heavy shopping bags she was lugging, loomed unex-
pectedly, boggled her eyes, and then quickened her
pace. A second tomato cast by the cheeky young lout
with the longish face stirred Polikarp Feofanovich
to an access of fury. Trying to shield himself, he had
fallen on to his backside and a few drops of urine had
spattered his trousers. He fastened his fly and marched
determinedly toward the entrance to the block. He
was not accustomed to climbing so many flights of
stairs (he lived on the ground floor) and was panting
and puffing like a locomotive. He pressed the button by a door covered with a thick layer of grime.
There was a feeble buzz followed by tomb-like silence.
He pressed the doorbell once again. At last, he heard
footfalls and a longish face peeked from behind the
half-opened door. It was a child with hollow cheeks
and a piercing gaze.

"Call your parents!" thundered the recently pensioned war veteran.

"My parents are at work and they don't allow me

to talk to strangers. Who are you?" asked the longish face with undissimulated surprise.

"That's a good one! What do you mean, you snot-nosed brat? You throw tomatoes at me and now you're playing dead in the maize field!"

Polikarp Feofanovich was foaming at the mouth with fury.

"If you don't leave, I'll call the police!" said the cheeky young lout primly, slamming the door in his face.

The recently pensioned war veteran was left standing there open-mouthed.

He descended the stairs wracked by an acute feeling of humiliation. He sensed that he would not be able to rid himself of this feeling even after the young hooligan's parents and school principal had been called to account.

At home, in his spacious three-room apartment, where, since the death of his wife, messiness had reigned, chronic disquiet took hold of him. He went to the toilet and strained at length to void his bladder, groaning because of the pain, and then he ate some mashed beans. His eyebrows bristling, he gulped down the medicaments prescribed by the urologist, and collapsed, exhausted and depressed, onto the bed that he wet night after night. For the first time, he was tormented by the feeling that he was too old to fight against injustice. With sadness, he realized that he himself had treated Veniamin Nikanorovich unjustly. Oblivion stole over him only after he had doped himself with sleeping pills. He dreamed a recurring, unpleasant dream, which always broke off before its finale.

He was at a funeral, in a building half-destroyed by bombardment. There was a coffin, on one side of which stood a child and a woman hunched with suffering, weeping, while on the other side stood Polikarp Feofanovich, as if on tenterhooks. From time to time, the woman and the child would pierce Polikarp Feofanovich with their eyes and say something to him in an accusing voice. But he could not make out the words. Overcoming his fear, Polikarp Feofanovich would slowly approach the coffin, in which was lying . . . stop! The dream would end abruptly, and the recently pensioned war veteran would awake, tortured by a fathomless terror that caused his heart to palpitate. This was how it had been for many years. But today, perhaps because of the sleeping pills, the dream took an even more terrifying turn. First of all, he was able to make out the words uttered by the haggard woman, who was talking to him in German, and he knew that the woman was declaring him guilty of the death of her husband. Then, the dream did not break off, as it usually did when he approached the coffin. As a result, he saw the corpse of a fascist in military uniform and he knew that it was the prisoner he had killed in 1944 as he was trying to escape. The fact that the fascist had had a child and a wife disturbed Polikarp Feofanovich. And as if this were not enough, the corpse of the fascist phantasmagorically metamorphosed into a child with a longish face, his eyes smoldering deep in their sockets, his face livid, who jumped out of the coffin and threw a rotten tomato at him, shouting at the top of his voice: "I'll call the police!"

Polikarp Feofanovich woke up in the depths of the night, writhing in the rumpled bedclothes. After his heart stopped hammering, he got out of bed and lit the lamp. He urinated on the floor before he could reach the bathroom. With bleary eyes, he tried in vain to find a pair of clean underpants among the clothes piled in a disordered heap within the wardrobe. He looked out of the window: the darkness outside was impenetrable. He sat down in an armchair, trying to define his indisposition. He had the feeling that he knew the hooligan with the longish face. Paradoxically, this impression grew stronger as he contemplated the mess in the bedroom. The revelation was both sudden and bewildering. In stupefaction, he realized that the hooligan was one of the well-wishing pioneers whom, a year before, the neighborhood Russian-Moldavian school had given the task of tidying up his apartment and doing his shopping.

The Devil take him! The pioneer with the longish face was a jovial, diligent child, a lad with a warm gaze. He could have sworn by him on his life. He clearly remembered that one day the longish face had helped him to beat all his carpets and clean his oven, and another time, after his impatient fellow pioneers had left, the lad had eagerly asked him to tell him stories about the glorious past. He had gazed avidly into Polikarp Feofanovich's eyes as the veteran told him about the cruelty of the Hitlerite invaders and the heroism of the Soviet soldiers, about the fierce battles in which he had taken part and, naturally, about the liberation of Soviet Moldavia. Thanks to this curious pioneer, who often interrupted him merely to beg him not to omit a single detail, Polikarp Feofanovich had felt once more a need to communicate, a need repressed for so long. How was it possible for such a well-behaved pioneer to turn into an insolent lout? How could the child who had once cleaned his apartment now throw rotten tomatoes at him? He had done nothing to offend him. On the contrary, more than once he had given him money to buy himself ice cream. It was clear that that child was not mentally abnormal, although the longish head might be a result of a hard childhood. But could the childhood of those pioneers, who lived in the era of developed socialism, really be regarded as being hard? Not a bit of it. Polikarp Feofanovich let out a deep sigh. His generation had had a childhood full of hardships.

Unbidden, an embarrassing situation came to his mind. He had once gone into a food shop where people were queuing for Doktorskaya sausages. He had gone straight to the counter, shouting, "I'm a veteran!" Weary, but respectful, the people had moved to one side. But a long-haired lout, wearing jeans, had not at all been impressed by his medals and had yelled at him furiously: "What do you think you're doing, pushing in! You think only you are a human being?" It is true that in the end the woman behind the counter and the people in the queue had put the impertinent lout in his place, but Polikarp Feofanovich had been out of sorts for the rest of the day. Straining his memory, the recently pensioned war veteran realized with consternation that he had been insulted and mocked on numerous occasions: on a trolley bus packed to the gills nobody had offered him a seat, but instead some schoolchildren had made fun of him, asking him in whiny voices whether his legs were aching; his newspapers used to vanish from his letterbox, which he would find stuffed with garbage; a neighbor, a lad in the Komsomol, whom he had scolded for scribbling on the walls of the landing, never used to bid him

good day; a gang of noisy ruffians playing the guitar
in front of the block not only ignored his protests but
also suggested that he should buzz off.

Little by little, the naked truth was emerging: the
younger generation was contaminated by indifference
and a lack of moral fiber. There was a multitude of
facts, all of which were eloquent in this respect. He
was gripped by a powerful, devouring fear. Pioneers
and Komsomol youth were disrespecting the war veterans who had shed their blood for them, but even
more frightening was the fact that society *did not
notice* this attitude. Those hooligans went unpunished! Consequently, society was sick.

Something serious had occurred. In appearance,
everything was as before, or even better than before,
because the enemies of the people had been annihilated and fear had been instilled in the foreign foes.
But there was no longer any drive, the enthusiasm of
the first five-year plans, or the proverbial wholesome-
ness of youth. These things had evaporated, in spite of
better standards of living. Or perhaps it was the very
absence of enemies and hardships that had caused this
moral decline? He rushed to the telephone and began
dialing the number of Veniamin Nikanorovich. He
immediately thought better of it, remembering that
it was the middle of the night. He went back to the
armchair and sank into his memories.

In the good old days, he had known different pioneers, wonderful children who used to work at the lathe and in the fields, help the families of those who were away fighting the war, give concerts in the hospitals, tend to the wounded, send parcels and letters to the soldiers at the front. Wherever those children might have been—behind the front line, far from the fighting, or even in the territory temporarily occupied by the enemy—they always loyally performed their duties as pioneers, cherishing their red cravats, doing everything in their power to hasten victory. The fascists would never have believed that Vladimir Kaznacheyev, the avenging pioneer who had blown up fifteen squadrons, was only fourteen. Thousands of young heroes had been decorated with medals. Pioneers Marat Kazey, Lyona Golikov, Zina Portnova and Valya Kotik had been declared Heroes of the Soviet Union post mortem, whereas the pioneers of today threw rotten tomatoes at your head and insulted you. Why did the parents and teachers of these children pretend nothing was happening? What would happen if the number of these insensitive individuals devoid of ideals were to increase continuously? His ears were ringing. He urinated once more. He set the alarm clock for seven o'clock and, taking some sleeping pills, dozed off.

In the morning, his pessimism had advanced so

far that he no longer wanted to go to the urologist who had prescribed his treatment. To be honest, since the day his wife died things had not been going well for the recently pensioned war veteran. The jokey, good-humored man had gradually become a wreck. He ate poorly, not having the patience to cook, and he began to hit the bottle, trying to rid himself of the disquiet that was gnawing away at him. But given that neither Russian vodka nor Moldavian wine agreed with him as well as they did in his youth, he had taken up fishing, with the help of Veniamin Nikanorovich. He gave up fishing after a violent attack of prostatitis, however. At first, he felt a diffuse and intermittent pain between his legs, then he started having to urinate frequently and, in time, the pain became unbearable, making urination difficult. For this reason, every night the silence in the apartment was broken by heart-rending groans, the shuffling of slippers and the gurgling of the sink. Finally, he plucked up courage and went to a polyclinic. Urologist Vasile Octavianovich, a rather tedious man, recommended antibiotics and vitamin E, but voiced his fear that, without massage of the prostate gland, these would not have the desired effect. And so Polikarp Feofanovich ended up a laughing-stock: here he was at a venerable age with someone sticking his finger up his arse. But Vasile Octavianovich was of the opinion that there was no shame in something that was for the benefit of one's health. Thereafter, he had plenty of time at his disposal: he rarely went out of the apartment, for fear of pissing himself in public; he would doze off in front of the television set; he played dominos with other war veterans; in an old trunk he found some yellowed photographs that he never tired of looking at. Unfortunately, the intolerable illness gave him no peace, in spite of him swallowing medicaments with great regularity. He grew irascible. Even Vasile Octavianovich was unsatisfied with the inefficacy of the course of treatment. One day, after another ritual session of massaging, the urologist asked him to try to clench his gland, and then he gazed thoughtfully at the embarrassed war veteran, without uttering a word. Just as the silence was growing unbearable, he finally spoke: "Polikarp Feofanovich, I am doing everything within my power to cure your illness. The antibiotics, vitamins and massage have reduced the inflammation of the prostate gland considerably, but . . . my impression is that the essential thing would be for you to contribute."

"Me to contribute?" Polikarp Feofanovich was baffled. "Don't I swallow all those nauseating tablets you prescribe me?"

"You haven't understood me. I know you are a widow. I am sorry to have to say it, but it is obvious that you need to have sexual relations, in other words, you need a woman . . ."

Polikarp Feofanovich gulped and took his leave, plunged in thought. He had not been with a woman since the death of his wife, and since the onslaught of the prostatitis he had been having increasingly fewer erections. Three or four nocturnal emissions a year were his entire joy. Sometimes he yearned for a woman. Not to tame his inflamed prostate gland, but to help him escape from the hideous loneliness. But who would want a knackered old man? There was, it was true, a middle-aged Moldavian woman, who sold vegetables at the neighborhood market, a divorced little woman from an outlying district of Kishinev, who glowed with joy whenever she saw Polikarp Feofanovich. The Moldavian woman did not ask him banal questions about his health or the weather, but about achievements and plans. When he talked to this woman, whose eyes expressed benevolence and esteem, the recently pensioned war veteran regained his confidence. The Moldavian woman had confessed to him everything about her failed marriage, being of the opinion that only a man of Polikarp Feofanovich's experience and authority could sift the wheat from the chaff and give her sound advice. The war veteran had listened to her attentively. He had taken her side. He had condemned the egregious boorishness of her

former husband and assured her that she had no reasons to feel sorry. Touched, the charming Moldavian
woman ate him up with her eyes. The next, natural
step was an exchange of visits. But he would have to
talk it over with his son in Odessa first. He telephoned
him one evening and, in a good mood, told his son
that he wanted to remarry. Oleg Polikarpovich, a very
busy engineer, jumped down his throat, demanding
he come to his senses: "You're thinking like a child,
Dad! That whore will string you along just so she can
get her hands on your apartment! Or maybe you've
forgotten that you have a grandson?" He had forgotten, it goes without saying. His son and grandson
only ever visited him at Easter and Christmas. They
never found the time even to telephone him. Polikarp
Feofanovich blew his top. What about them? They
had abandoned him, leaving him alone and helpless,
and now they were foaming at the mouth because of
the apartment? Wasn't it rather his son and daughter-
in-law who were the ones who could hardly wait for
him to die?

And was losing the apartment really more terrifying than loneliness?

He remained out of sorts after the day he spoke to
his son. He rarely left the house, spending most of his
time thinking about the meaning of life. He had been
late in discovering the charms of rumination. His life

up until retirement had been a headlong race. He had
never found the time for reflection. Now, he was no
longer sure whether he had been truly happy or not.
It was a matter of fact that he had achieved much:
he had crushed the fascist beast, taking part in the
storming of the Reichstag; he had ploughed Kazakh
celery fields; he had worked in the City Communist
Party Committee and obtained an apartment in the
Ryshkanovka district. But the sudden death of his
wife, the prostatitis, his retirement, loneliness and,
above all, the moral decay of society's youth had
plunged him into the depths of despair . . .

When, at the demand of Veniamin Nikanorovich,
the neighbors had broken the door down, the corpse
of the recently pensioned war veteran was in an
advanced state of putrefaction. The overwhelming
stench caused many to vomit and take to their heels.
In his friend's hand, Veniamin Nikanorovich found
a yellowed photograph: Polikarp Feofanovich, his
wife, and little Oleg, arm in arm next to the statue of
Lenin in the centre of Kishinev. Ten people came to
the funeral: six war veterans, two neighbors, a bored
political instructor from the City Communist Party
Committee, and a middle-aged woman wearing a
headscarf, who was sobbing loudly. Caught up in the
whirl of day-to-day life, the son arrived in Kishinev
two days later and, before going to the cemetery,

he examined the empty apartment carefully. In the kitchen, a tomato left on the windowsill was emanating a nauseating miasma.

The Dream of Ionel Pîslari

EATEN AWAY BY RUST, the hot water pipe had burst in the middle of the night. They had all known it would burst, but nobody had lifted a finger to prevent the accident.

"Damn it to hell!"

Enervated by insomnia, Ionel Pîslari leapt up from his creaking, ramshackle sofa bed, groped for his undervest, softly opened the door to his room and went out onto the long, dark, fourth-floor landing. The communal kitchen quickly filled with water and steam. It looked like a geyser zone. Woken by the bang, the disgusted faces of a few tenants were peeking from around the doors to their rooms.

"Who's making all that noise, *blya*?"[1] yelled Vasya

---

[1] Russian expletive (*блядь*), whose literal meaning is "whore" — *Translator's note.*

the electrician, a burly man whom it was inadvisable to upset.

"A *truba*[2] burst in the kitchen! We need to turn the water off!" exhorted Ionel Pîslaru.

"Fuck your *truba*!" exclaimed Vasya, frothing with fury, and went back to bed.

There were only two other conscientious individuals who did not follow his example. Flooding the kitchen, the reddish-brown, chlorinated water was now gushing down the hall. They rushed to stop the breach with a rag, but leapt back the next instant, howling in pain. The water was boiling. They rushed downstairs and timidly knocked on the door of the superintendent. A bellicose man, after swearing at them till he was blue in the face and calming his wife, deprived of a much-craved orgasm for the umpteenth time, the superintendent tossed them a bunch of keys and slammed the door in their face. They stood motionless for two or three minutes and then, coming to their senses, dashed down to the basement, where, among the junk, feces and ceaselessly dripping pipes, there scurried rats so fearsome that they put even the cats to flight. Plucking up courage, they pushed open the heavy door, on which someone had scrawled in chalk, *Bei bykov! Vsem sosati!*[3] and *Long live rock 'n' roll!* They

---

[2] Russian: "pipe."

[3] Russian: "Beat the yokels! Suck it all of you!"

groped for around half an hour in the pitch darkness, tripping up and thinking of the beds they had been forced to abandon. Finally, just as they were losing patience, they detected a sack of rotten potatoes next to a moldy wall. Ionel Pîslari climbed up on the sack and—braced by his "teammates" made weak by the exertion and the fetid odors—he stretched out his arm and with difficulty twisted the stopcock, shutting off the restive hot water. He then returned to his room, where his wife Lyuba and two children were sleeping the sleep of the dead, and, exhausted, disgusted, flung himself back down on the ramshackle foldout arm-chair. He remained awake the whole night, from time to time pressing his ear against the thin wall, through which seeped the groans of a woman in heat.

"They were fucking in the midst of a flood!" were the words that went through his head toward morn-ing, before loud bangs turned the cancerous bowels of the hostel inside out.

The plumbers arrived three days later, they patched the pipe, knocked back the wine provided by the tenants, said something about the need to look after national property, and left, staggering as they went.

Ionel Panteleyevich Pîslari was nearing the age of forty and had worked for years as a porter at the Vibropribor factory. In his youth, he had been a vil-lage cowherd, after which, tempted by the mysterious life of the city, he had come to Kishinev and for a time unloaded goods at the railroad station. He had commuted from the village until the day he married Lyuba—a hard-working, decent peasant woman who, in addition, had a thirteen-square-metre room in the Meat Packing Plant workers' hostel on Strada Muncești. But the feeling that God had given him a leg up and the unbridled passion of the honeymoon gradually disintegrated under the monotony of everyday life. In the drab hostel, without balconies, populated by the uncouth, the prematurely decrepit, the sallow, the anemic, there reigned a stifling atmosphere devoid of all eroticism. To the very right of the door to their tiny room was the door to the communal toilet, so dark that you couldn't see your hand in front of your face and could easily step in a puddle of piss, followed by the door to the communal washroom, the sill of whose painted-out windowpane was covered in cigarette butts and burnt matches, and then the door to the communal kitchen, where day and night soup seethed and kettles boiled, for the simple reason that the greasy gas stove had only two burners. A clothes line over the stove, from which hung socks and underpants imbued with the smell of soup, testified to the narrow washroom's incapacity to compensate for the lack of balconies. Clothes hung outside sometimes vanished.

Bilious, sweating women queued to fry eggs, scrub laundry at the washboard, reduce the mountain of dirty dishes in the sink. They quarreled with the housewives from the floors below, who climbed the stairs in the hope of finding a free sink, they yelled at the noisy, boisterous children who raced along the corridor and frequently came down with diarrhea, they battled the hail of cockroaches that mounted full-frontal assaults on the pots and pans of food. The piercing, pestilential stench of boiled onion/bleach/urine/borsht, which turned your stomach, and the noise of the flushing toilet forced Ionel Pîslari to pad his door. The labor was in vain! The feeling that he was living in a passageway did not diminish in the slightest.

Nor were the surroundings of the hostel conducive to a feeling of wellbeing. It was an outlying, impoverished district, the architecture was bleak: identical-looking, overcrowded hostels, a dismal food store, a tavern where savage fights used to break out, garbage skips next to which stray dogs mated, a twenty-four-hour pharmacy whose regular customers bought nothing but valerian, aspirin and penicillin for themselves and hematogen and vitamin C for their children, and, at the city's very edge, crumbling sheds, warehouses, a depot, and a row of garages. Here and there grinned open manholes, pipelines sprouted from the earth dripping dirty water, and along the bumpy, winding road constantly rattled dump trucks, concrete mixers, mechanical diggers, which shook the hostels worse than an earthquake. The streets were mostly deserted, if you didn't count the gangs of children, who, once they got bored of scouring the neighborhood to collect old iron and waste paper, went around deflating the tires of the cars or played toss the rock. Sometimes they would break the windows of the hostel tenants, who reacted violently. An incensed adult had once hit a rock-throwing child over the head with a frying pan, and the child had had to have an operation.

It was after the birth of his daughter Ludmila that Ionel Pîslari first had the feeling that the family raft was adrift. The evenings when he and his wife had walked hand in hand to the Moscow Cinema to see the latest tear-jerking Indian film had faded from memory. His wife had grown irascible and hectored him to help her when she got back home, broken with exhaustion: He had to help her wash and iron diapers, to get up in the night to soothe the crying baby girl and change her, to buy all kinds of medicaments and vitamins that weren't available at their local pharmacy. After their son Ruslan was born, it became more and more common for them not to have grocery money, and in their thirteen-square-metre room, you couldn't so much as turn around without bumping into something. There were constant arguments for the flimsiest reasons. Once, Lyuba had given him a tongue-lashing ostensibly because he'd gone into the communal kitchen wearing his patched long johns, which certainly put a smile on the faces of the otherwise dour housewives. But the real reason had been that the envelope in which they painstakingly put aside money soon emptied. He would clash with his wife at the drop of a hat. Lyuba pilfered hash, hotdog sausages, and pastrami from the meat packing plant and asked him in a grief-stricken voice why he didn't do anything to support the family. But what more could he do? He worked his fingers to the bone, having finally found himself a second job. After a carrying loads all day at the factory, he went to the railroad station to do the same. He would get back home late at night, exhausted, in a foul mood, he would lie down on the extensible armchair, trying not to make a noise, lest he wake his wife and children asleep on the extensible couch alongside, and he would fix his eyes on a spider's web as a miserable fear crept into his soul. He no longer knew: it was quite possible that he didn't love his wife. Lyuba had metamorphosed into an obese woman with a double chin, who kept him on a tight leash and counted his every mouthful of food. They had long since stopped planning for the future.

He would toss and turn until dawn. Sometimes he

would press his ear to the peeling wall and, gritting his teeth, attentively listen to the voluptuous moans of the woman in the next room. On the nights when there was nothing to be heard, he would tiptoe to the window and gaze blankly for hours through the clammy pane at the outline of a distant tower block under construction, flanked by two cranes. The thought that they too might one day have an apartment in such a block exceeded his power of imagination. But it was not impossible. Even Vova Ciocan the machinist—a kind-hearted *patsan*,[4] who used to buy him a drink when Lyuba had gone through his pockets, leaving them empty—had a forty-one-square-metre (!) apartment in the Ryshkanovka district. Lately, Ionel had grown irritated at the fact that Vova always used to complain about what a hard life he had. At the weekend, they would escape from their families, go to a smoke-filled tavern, where they ordered a strong Xeres and, while Vova reeled off his troubles, Ionel would mostly stare into space.

That Sunday, which he was to remember countless times, down to the smallest detail, an ordinary enough occurrence shattered his peasant optimism once and for all; it drove him out of his mind. He had joined the lads playing dominos in the yard of the hostel. They

---

[4] Russian: "lad, bloke."

were slamming their dominos down on the peeling table, savoring their Zhiguli beer. On a transistor radio, they were listening to a rousing speech by a writer of the people. Or rather Ionel Pîslari was listening, since the others were chattering about this and that.

The writer of the people said that the proposed new Constitution coincided with the sixtieth anniversary of the Great October victory, that since then a powerful country had been built, founded on new principles, a country that led the world when it came to the production of material and spiritual goods, a country that represented the shared interests of every layer of society, a country of progress and peace, a country with a new morality, communist morality, to which man's exploitation of his fellow man was alien, a country of free labor, of collective labor, a country of collectivism. The writer also said that the proposed Constitution pointed the way to a higher level in the ascent toward communism and that that was why it was being presented to the working class for their examination and approbation, that the whole country would be made cognizant of the proposal, would examine it thoroughly, and that each citizen would contribute his opinions and suggestions to the discussion about society's Fundamental Law.

Ionel Pîslari had had no idea about the proposed Constitution and he found it hard to believe that the sweaty, beer-addled men around him could possibly have any suggestions to make. All of a sudden, a glossy black Volga sped into the yard, raising a choking cloud of dust, honking deafeningly and putting an end to the chatter and the clack of dominos. No sooner had the car braked than a stunning long-legged blonde in a low-cut blue dress emerged from the entrance to the hostel and walked over to it. It was Veronica Lapteacru,[5] the Moldavian literature teacher: the neighbor whose nocturnal moans and creaking bed-springs so troubled Ionel Pîslari. A natty bigwig wearing dark glasses jumped out of the car and opened the passenger door, helping Veronica to insert her mouthwateringly long legs. The wisecracking dominos players were left speechless, gazing after the Volga as it sped away. When the cloud of dust lifted, the thunderous voice of a corpulent housewife, who was beating her carpets nearby, helped them regain their senses: "What are you lot ogling at? You've got nothing but whores and booze on your brains!"

The blood rushed to Ionel's face.

"Shut your gob!" yelled Vasya the machinists, causing her to take to her heels.

Discombobulated, they resumed their favorite pastime.

---

[5] Lapteacru, literally "sour milk" — *Translator's note*

"Uppity bitch! Fucks the *nachalniki*,[6] she does!" remarked a laborer who constantly chewed his nails, after taking a slug of beer and heaving a deep sigh.

"Drooling after her, aren't you? Set your sights lower, you *muzhik*.[7] She's too classy for you. But then again, it's not just the *nachalniki* who've humped her, if you catch my drift," said Vasya the machinist, teasing him, although you could tell from his face that he wasn't all that sure of himself.

The nail-chewing laborer was left utterly deflated and, while all the others gazed at him dumbly, as if he were some kind of exotic exhibit, Ionel Pîslari felt a gnawing pain in his heart. For the first time ever, he was filled with a repulsive, rancid envy, an envy that welled from some unfathomable emptiness of his being. The scales fell from his eyes in an instant: life in the real sense of the world, life and all that was precious about it, was passing him by; it shunned him like a fresh young girl shunning a slobbering old man. He was filled with disgust at the chucklehead who gnawed his nails, at the coarse fitter, at the corpulent housewife who had railed at them, and above all at his own impotence, which was abruptly thrown into relief, making a mockery of him. He stood up stiffly, flung away his dominos, to the astonishment of his

---

[6] Russian: "bosses" (i.e. high-ranking Communist Party officials) — *Translator's note*

[7] Russian: "peasant" — *Translator's note*

pals, and quickly strode away, not knowing where he was going.

He had cooled off somewhat by the time he reached the tavern, which emanated a familiar stench. He was hesitant to press the filthy door handle: he wasn't in the habit of lubricating his throat all by himself. Finally, he went inside, having been given a shove by his seething envy, and ordered a bottle of Xeres. After rummaging through every pocket, he then ordered another. He sipped the sherry slowly, in a corner that the weak light bulb was too faint to illumine, staring at the images flickering soundlessly on the ramshackle television set. From time to time, the images would disappear, whereupon the sour waitress would bang her fist on the television set, which had miraculously carried on working for many a year. Although he felt a gnawing in the pit of his stomach, he finally drained the two bottles, which left him well and truly drunk. Although he had no more money, he sat there until evening, dozing off and jolting awake at each bang of the fist on the television set. Finally, the asphyxiating tobacco smoke and the loud cursing of the raucous drinkers, who in the meantime had been arriving in increasing numbers, forced him to leave.

No sooner had he opened the door to his tiny room, no sooner had he managed to say he was starving hungry, than Lyuba, her hair in rollers, took him to task. She vociferated, gesticulated, her hair rollers jiggling, begged him to stop drinking and think of his family, of his children's future—they went to school wearing rags and tatters and had ended up bottom of their classes. He gazed in amazement at the dopey boy wearing a coat with holes in the elbows and at the slatternly, tastelessly made-up girl, and he was hard put to recognize his own son and daughter. How had he not noticed (they had been crammed together in the one thirteen-square-metre room for years and years!) that Ruslan and Ludmila had changed so radically? What astonished him was not that they had grown up so suddenly but that they were such strangers to him.

"Why don't you take care of your clothes, snot-nose!" yelled Ionel Pîslari, rushing to give the lad a clout across the lugs.

Lyuba planted herself in front of him: "You've drunk yourself senseless by the looks of it! How about you tell us when was the last time you bought him a shirt! All you're capable of doing is boozing with all the other failures!"

His wife's snarling mouth stank of garlic, and her hair rollers were bouncing up and down, making her look ridiculous.

"Suck my dick, you stinking whore!" roared Ionel Pîslari, abruptly losing all discernment and punching her in the face.

He had never hit her before. In the same instant, blood spurted from her nose and the children's eyes, bulging in terror, riveted him to the spot. He was gripped by sudden, overwhelming remorse.

Lyuba and the children packed their things and at the break of day, they left for the country, even before the Soviet national anthem could stirringly resound from the belly of the decrepit radio set. Ionel Pîslari sat up in bed, and grimly observed that—as one might expect—there were no sandwiches or hot tea waiting for him. He swore furiously. His head was spinning. He felt he had reached a crossroads in life, but he also had an acute sense of his own smallness, amplified by his utter inability to come to any decision.

After the official news, read by a professional-sounding voice, there was a report on the meeting that had taken place between the collective farm workers of Doibany[8] village and the most important writer of the people in the Soviet Socialist Republic of Moldavia. The living literary classic had confessed to the workers that he wrote his novels in such a way that the reader *"would realize that every Soviet man plays an important role in the life of society, in the advancement of the power of the Homeland, in the*

---

[8] Literally "Tuppence" — *Translator's note*

struggle for the victory of Leninist ideas." Ionel pricked up his ears. To him, writers were idlers, chatterers who talked drivel. But even so, they piqued his curiosity, representing as they did a profession that was enigmatic, superior, inaccessible.

He slowly got up, hunched from the chronically sore muscles that had wracked him for years. He furiously rummaged in the cupboard, without finding the envelope with the money. He looked all around the room, peered under the couch, swore, opened the rickety refrigerator and studied its contents in disgust: an egg, a few jars of leftovers, *a rotten tomato*, a tuft of shriveled dill, some pickled cucumbers. He looked at the clock: he would never make it to the factory if he attempted to fry the egg in the kitchen where the housewives were now swarming. He gobbled the cucumbers and grimly left for work, as if setting off to war.

WRITER B. I.:
> *A family of working men are we,*
> *In the evening with Lenin we chat,*
> *With him we set out at break of day,*
> *Our overalls streaming through the land.*

He toiled the whole day, burdened by the thought that he no longer meant anything to his wife and children. How had Lyuba come to hold him in such contempt?

A harebrained idea passed through his mind: he would be able to regain his wife's love and compassion only if he died in a terrible accident. But what was he supposed to do? Commit suicide? To hell with that!

At around midnight, as he was fumbling with his key in the lock, Veronica Lapteacru emerged from the washroom with a towel over her shoulder. She came to a stop next to Ionel, delicate and enticing. She leaned her angelic little head close to the ashen mug of the man, who was taken by surprise, and whispered: "I couldn't care less what the other louts who live here think, but I couldn't bear the thought of you, Ion Panteleyevich, taking their side!"

For a fraction of a second, the blushing schoolmistress and the bewildered porter studied each other with their eyes. Coming out of the communal kitchen, a somnolent, slatternly housewife stared at them as if they were enemies of the people.

"Lyuba packed her bags . . . She wants a divorce," muttered Ionel Pîslari.

"Ion Panteleyevich, I can't believe it! Hmm, yes . . . I'm sorry, really I am . . . How about we talk? I'll make you a cup of tea. What do you say?"

The schoolmistress's warm gaze reminded him of times long past. Yes, that was the way Lyuba used to look at him during their honeymoon. Downcast, he mumbled something unintelligible.

"I'll go and put the kettle on . . ." said Veronica
casually, interpreting in her own way the porter's
disconcertion.

With slow steps she entered the adjacent room,
leaving the door ajar. Ionel Pîslaru was left gasping
for breath. Finally taking a grip on himself, he opened
the thickly padded door of his own room and, without turning on the light, slumped in the extensible
armchair, which creaked from every joint.

He pondered the schoolmistress's proposal, examining it on every side. He didn't know what to do.
Veronica Lapteacru had little by little become his life's
obsession. He went weak at the knees when, on the
other side of the thin wall, the woman with the long
legs let out a long moan. At the factory, he forgot
about his toil thinking about her, trying to fathom
whom she was sleeping with. Naturally, there was
that nonchalant bigwig, who'd once looked him up
and down as if he were some kind of chucklehead.
But the bigwig—whom he'd loathed from that day
hence—never entered the tenement. One morning,
waiting his turn outside the toilet cubicle, he'd see
Vasya the machinist slowly emerge from Veronica's
room. He'd been left gobsmacked when the oafish
machinist gave him a friendly wink. Could a beautiful
woman, courted by a *nachalnik*, really be having it off
with an ape like that? It was inconceivable. But since

his neighbor's nocturnal moans were incessant, Ionel Pîslaru often found himself crushed by his suffering.

They said she was nothing but a two-bit whore. The housewives gossiped about her all day long as they cooked in the communal kitchen. The men gossiped about her as they played dominos. The young boys gossiped about her as they kicked their heels outside the building, struggling to solve the mystery of their first wet dreams. The women despised her and secretly envied her. The men despised her and secretly desired her. The young boys despised her and saw her in their dreams night after night. Ionel Pîslaru's feelings were much more confused, harder to define. The only thing for certain was that he didn't despise her. It was no accident that he became grumpy and irritable when the domino players spoke ill of her.

Only an idiot would not have noticed the blatant difference between the chubby, sallow, cantankerous Lyuba and the slender-waisted, feline schoolmistress, who dressed so elegantly, so expensively. Did Lyuba paint her nails? He'd never seen his wife do that in all the years he'd known her! And there was another thing. Although arrogant in her dealings with the tenants who despised her, Veronica smiled at him sweetly and seemed ready to talk about his life whenever he bumped into her. She was always attentive to his children: she gave them candies, fountain pens, books, and even small change, much to Lyuba's chagrin.

His slatternly wife insisted that he "avoid that whore so that people's tongues won't start wagging."

One day, the schoolmistress had helped Ionel Pîslaru's daughter to write a composition on the subject of labor. Even though he didn't have a clue about what his children studied at school, Ionel Pîslaru had displayed an unexpected interest in that composition written by his neighbor. He read, "In the old days, labor did not make man happy, because it was not a free and willing pursuit—for centuries men had to toil for the benefit of the masters who oppressed them—such labor brought no joy—it was a curse, a scourge—but after the victory of the Great October Socialist Revolution, the factories, the land, all the country's wealth passed into the hands of the people—the workers became the masters in their own country—the workers and the peasants are no longer forced to break their backs so that the capitalists can lead a life of leisure, but work for themselves and for the good of the entire nation—this is why people have radically changed their attitude to labor, they have begun to view it in a creative way—labor has become a necessity, a calling, which sometimes leads men of labor to commit true acts of heroism." The difficulty of reading it—Ionel was barely literate—stirred an ambiguous feeling in him. The ideas were commonplace,

somehow bewildering, ideas with which everybody
was familiar, but not everybody could express them.
It was startlingly obvious the schoolmistress was an
intellectual. How could such a well-read woman live
in a hostel like that?

Ionel Pîslari hesitated. He felt attracted to the lis-
some schoolmistress and at the same time he was wary
of her, as if mindful of his wife's interdictions. He lost
his head whenever he saw her and went around all day
like a wet turkey. His eyesight had suddenly become
sharper. For example, once he was surprised to notice
that his son's hair was long. He raged at him, even
though Ruslan had been growing his hair for a whole
year. His eyes fell on his wife's faded, frayed apron,
and their carelessly disguised mutual recriminations
erupted once more.

Someone was tapping on the radiator pipe. He knew
it was Veronica. He plucked up courage. He hesitated
in front of the half-open door, wiped his feet on the
mat, and timidly stepped over the threshold. Perhaps
due to the cleanliness and the tidiness of the expensive
items therein, the identical thirteen-square-metres on
the other side of the wall seemed more spacious, air-
ier. He stared at the Polish-made bed, then at the
painting hanging on the wall, which depicted the toil
of some bearded bargemen, the huge crystal vase; he
gazed in amazement at the East-German record player,

the shelves groaning under the "weight" of Soviet literature, the Persian rug underfoot, the armchair in
which the pensive woman was lolling . . . Veronica
invited him to sit down. She settled her head com-
fortably on the backrest of the armchair and began
to speak, her eyes boring into him.

"I care about you, Ion Panteleyevich, not because
you're my neighbor, but because you're a decent
person, the only decent person in the whole of this
wretched hostel. I've been wanting to talk to you for
a long time and if I understand rightly, the time has
come for me to give you some advice. Is it true that
you and Lyuba want to get divorced?"

He cleared his throat, but rather than speak up, he
merely nodded his head.

"And is this what you, Ion Panteleyevich, intend
to do?"

He mumbled something, chewing his lips.
Veronica knitted her brows.

"I know, Ion Panteleyevich, that you have a hard
time and that you're always quarrelling. I'm hardly
blind! But if you divorce *now*, you'll find yourself
in an even harder situation! Where will you live and
how will you pay for your *sustenance*? What will the
children do without a father? Think also about the
fact that you *will not be viewed well!*"

He hadn't thought about it. From the hall came

hoarse voices: some housewives were conversing about their digestive upsets.

"I've spoken about you to Yuri Pavlovich. I told him that you're an energetic man, politically sound, but overlooked. He promised me he would help you, but you mustn't divorce, at least *not for the time being*. You'll be a Party member, then an activist. The factory will find another porter. When the time is right, Yuri Pavlovich will pave the way and you'll receive an apartment. Aren't you sick of this hostel? I'm not joking, Ion Panteleyevich! Let this remain between ourselves: I'll be moving into a two-room apartment in two weeks! You can obtain an apartment, too. All you have to do is do what Yuri Pavlovich tells you. He's highly influential and, you know how it is, Ion Panteleyevich, even the most talented people need a protector . . ."

Veronica stretched lazily, looking through her half-closed eyelashes at Ionel Pîslari, whose temples were throbbing. His mind was far away. Finally, he spoke, articulating the words with difficulty: "Veronica Andreyevna, I can't believe my ears . . . You're so good to me . . . I too . . . care about you! But I don't know whether I can live with Lyuba any more and I don't think she'll ever come back . . ."

Somebody was stamping loudly down the hall.

"She'll come back if you ask her, Ion Panteleyevich.

There's nothing more changeable than the weather and women. You won't have to suffer a lifetime, but *now* is not the time to divorce. And there's another thing I want to tell you, Ion Panteleyevich . . ."

For a few minutes they both remained silent. Veronica raised one leg and studied it, seemingly forgetting all about Ionel Pîslari's presence. It was a long leg, white, fresh, the skin unusually soft for a woman who lived in such a hostel. Ionel felt the clean smell of soap envelop him. Veronica always smelled of imported soap, and not only immediately after she took a shower. Her bathrobe set off her full, provocative breasts. Inexplicably, Ionel found himself kneeling by her armchair, passionately kissing her foot. It all happened in a flash. Veronica gave a long moan and interlaced her fingers behind her neck.

That night, after he fell asleep, exhausted, in Veronica's bed, Ionel Pîslari had a terrifying dream. Lyuba burst through the door, disheveled, holding a sack of potatoes. From the gloom of the corridor behind her peeped the children, wide-eyed. Veronica shrugged, as if disclaiming responsibility. Naked, Ionel leapt to his feet. The hair stood up on his head. He looked into the dark-ringed eyes of his wife and understood that all was lost . . .

The Arrival of Grisha Furdui

THE WEARY TRAIN, packed to the gills, quaked before coming to a standstill. Easing its suffering, it spewed its guts on the platform of Kishinev station. A raucous, addled, motley crowd swarmed from the greasy carriages, emanating a fetid odor. Viewed from aloft, the train looked like a purulent caterpillar. The city, sweltering in the dog-day heat, strained to ingurgitate the mass of peasants laboring under their burdens.

Grisha Furdui alone remained rooted to the spot, contemplating in amazement the sun-drenched vista of the city, the grandeur of the edifice on whose frontispiece, beneath the clock, were emblazoned the words *ГАРА ВОКЗАЛ*, the endless expanse of asphalt. He had never seen so much asphalt and—as his worn shoes gingerly accustomed themselves to the solidity of the platform—to his mind the all too familiar images of the dirt roads of Tîrșița returned with intolerable acuity.

"Folk here don't have to waste money on cobbling!" This truth, which suddenly revealed itself to him, troubled him not only because it aroused his envy, but also because, despite its obviousness, it had been concealed from him for so long. He finally came to his senses, but arriving in the small square in front of the station, he was struck with amazement yet again. He stared for a long while at the sparkling fountain, around which chubby children with unusually white skin were running, and at the tall post upon which, like a flower atop a stalk, rested the arms of the Soviet Union, framed by the petals of the fifteen sister republics.

He let his eyes slowly travel around the square and, espying two metal booths around which people were crowding, he realized that he was painfully thirsty and soaked in sweat. He hesitated for a few moments: should he rush to the both inscribed *KBAC*, surrounded by women and children, or the one that said *ПИВО*, where only men were queuing? *Pivo*, naturally! He wasn't a bairn! After waiting his turn for half an hour, he slurped down the cold beer, filled with boundless satisfaction.

"How *zayebis*"[9] it would be if they brought some

---

[9] Russian slang: "fucking awesome."

pivo and *kvass* booths to Tîrşiţa!" he said to himself, giving free rein to his imagination. He ordered another mug, downing it in a single gulp and then belching loudly.

A middle-aged woman, who had just finishing drinking her kvass, gave him a look of insulting pity from above her spectacles.

He abruptly remembered that he hadn't come to Kishinev to idle around. He thrust his weather-beaten hands in the pockets of his faded sports jacket and rummaged there. Just as he was about to lose patience, his stiff fingers finally detected the greasy scrap of paper. He unfolded it and read aloud, syllable by syllable: *U-LI-TSA MUN-CHESHT-SKA-YA CHE-TY-RE.*[10] It was the street he had to find. In a workers' hostel of the famed Meat Plant lived his cousin, Ionel Pîslari.

Next to him, some lads with long hair, open shirts, and blue jeans were savoring the frothy beer. They were tearing strips from a huge smoked fish, belching without caring who might hear them, talking animatedly, chortling loudly. Grisha Furdui went up to them, timidly said hello, and asked them, mangling the Russian words, where Mun-chesht-ska-ya street was. The lads carried on talking, without paying any

---

[10] Russian: "4, Munceşti Street."

attention to him. Were they deaf? Had he not said it clearly enough? He apologized for bothering them and put the same question once more, more loudly this time.

The lively conversation stopped mid-sentence. In surprise, the long-haired lads turned their heads toward him and studied him carefully for a good couple of minutes, as if he were an extra-terrestrial. They looked him up and down, from head to foot.

The bag in which he had hurriedly stuffed a hen, a chunk of sheep's cheese, and a jug of wine began swaying back and forth in his hand. He was at a loss as to whether or not he should walk away.

All of a sudden, as if at a signal, the lads started laughing their heads off. They were neighing with laughter, splitting their sides, like idiots, forgetting about the beer, the smoked fish, everything else. Tears of laughter were streaming down their faces; they could barely stand up.

"*Ya okhuyevayu, muzhiki!*"[11] yelled a freckled lad, his voice hoarse from the beer and his raucous laughter.

Grisha Furdui couldn't understand a word of it. Unconsciously more than anything else, he began to feel a certain unease and took a step backward.

---

[11] Russian: "I'm gobsmacked, lads!"

"*Sbrey usy, papasha! I nauchisi govorit' normal'no!*"[12] yelled another of the lads and Grisha Furdui regretted not speaking Russian fluently.

His moustache? Why didn't they like his bushy moustache, which attracted the gaze of every woman in the village? he wondered in consternation as he walked away from those strange lads, who still hadn't stopped laughing. He touched his moustache and, somewhat to his surprise, found that it was drooping.

But his astonishment attenuated his disquiet as soon as he saw a magnificent skyscraper towering over the swarming cityscape, whose windows each reflected the blinding sun.

"What a marvel!" he said to himself, fascinatedly counting the floors of the hotel and completely forgetting about the eccentric long-haired lads.

All of a sudden, the city revealed itself to him in all its splendor, overwhelming him, throwing into relief his bucolic ignorance. He was wide-eyed: along the asphalted road—on either side of which there were rows of housing blocks, food stores, kiosks, telephone booths, carbonated water vending machines—there passed an endless procession of trolleybuses, buses, Zhigulis, Moskviches, and graceful Volgas.

The image of the rumbling carts back in Tîrșița

---

[12] "Shave that moustache off, daddy! And learn to talk properly!"

came to his mind. True, there were a few tractors in the village, which scattered suffocating black smoke, and two ramshackle Zaporozhets cars, driven by the chairman of the village soviet and the director of the cow farm. But there were certainly no telephone booths or soft drinks vending machines. There was a single telephone in the whole village—the one at the post office—and you had to wait all day long for your turn to phone Kishinev. As for sparkling fountains, they had wells instead, whose water was rather brackish and bad for the kidneys. But you didn't have any choice in the matter.

Staring at the passing automobiles, he was reminded of the poem declaimed by a Writer of the People who had once visited Tîrşiţa cow farm:

> From shivering, dark huts
> To sputniks and crystal palaces.
> A forward surge
> From the creaking cart
> To hundreds of horse power.

He couldn't remember the name of that writer, whose ostentatiously familiar manner had not seemed to betoken sincerity, but the poem had remained imprinted on his mind, despite the fact that he had flunked school. The poem had been a story that both enchanted and troubled him. To his stupefaction, he now realized that the story was true.

He was sweating so heavily that he rushed to a nearby vending machine, inserted a few coins, impatiently pressed the button, knocked back a few cups of gassy water, and belched boorishly.

Finally, a bored woman selling sunflower seeds informed him that he could get to Muncheshtskaya street on trolleybus number five. He headed in the direction of the stop, wondering why he had chosen to wear his sweat-sticky sports jacket.

Some of the people he passed stared at him in a fashion he found embarrassing.

In the yard of the hostel, with bottles of beer in front of them, a group of sweating men were playing dominos, whacking the pieces down onto the table and talking loudly.

"This lot have got it easy!" Grisha Furdui said to himself, trying in vain to quell the envy which, now that it had been awakened, kept prodding him harder and harder. Why the hell couldn't he get away from his chores to play dominos on a Sunday?

Walking past them, Grisha Furdui said hello. None of them deigned to notice him, apart from a burly man with an unhealthy-looking face, who gave him a sidelong glance.

He climbed the stairs, dimly lit by a bulb encased in juiceless flies, frozen for all eternity in the cobwebs.

Anesthetized by the smell of rural dung, his nostrils avidly inhaled the comforting reek of boiled onion, borsht, urine, chlorine.

By the door to the communal kitchen, he froze for a few seconds: a shapely woman with an impressive bosom was frying an omelet. He immediately recalled his bony, shriveled wife, with a bitter feeling of dissatisfaction and disappointment. Another detail that added to his bad mood was the two-ring gas cooker. Whereas he had a stove fueled with brushwood and wood chippings.

Swollen by the beer and gassy water, his kidneys forced him to tear his eyes away from the woman cooking, who looked like the incarnation of the life-force itself. He entered the dark latrine, treading on burnt matchsticks, blood-soaked tampons, and sticky bits of paper. As he pissed with intermittent flow, somebody was straining in the next cubicle, prompting a new revelation: during winter, the tenants of the hostel could shit in comfort, whereas he had to freeze his arse off in the rudimentary outhouse at the bottom of the garden.

The door to his cousin's room was ajar and Grisha Furdui entered without knocking. Looking up at the ceiling with his arms folded underneath his head, Ionel Pîslaru was lying on an extraordinary armchair-bed. "Cheers, Vanya!" said Grisha Furdui, greeting him, but his cousin did not so much as flinch. He seemed pensive. Should he shake him? Rather puzzled, Grisha Furdui sat down on the only chair in the thirteen-square-metre room, wondering what to do next.

The loud buzzing of the refrigerator instantly shattered his conviction that the damp atmosphere of his moss-ridden cellar was the ideal place for storing food. What the hell! Didn't the meat left in his cellar go off within just two days? Didn't his vegetables shrivel in just two weeks? No doubt about it, the refrigerator was a different kettle of fish! "I wonder how much a machine like that costs?" he asked himself, fidgeting in his chair.

As his cousin showed no sign of life, Grisha Furdui began to feel the full effect of the beer he'd ingurgitated, which the summer heat and his tiredness were amplifying considerably. When Ionel Pîslaru finally sat up, the messenger of rural eternity was dozing with the bag in his lap.

"Grisha! What the hell are you doing here?"

Not only was Ionel Pîslaru hungover, but he made no effort to disguise his dismay at the unexpected arrival of his relative. Grisha Furdui gave a start.

"Cheers, Vanya! I saw you were asleep and so I had a wee kip, too . . ."

"I wasn't asleep. I was thinking. What brings you here? You didn't tell me you were coming . . ."

There was a distinct note of reproach in Ionel Pîslaru's voice.

"I wanted to phone you, but the telephone at the post office was out of order. I want to buy myself an overcoat from your Universal Store, Vanya! I saved up the money and said to myself, 'Let's buy something decent.' I want you to help me choose an overcoat, Vanya, you're a city man, you know what's what, whereas this is my first time in Kishinev. I don't know nowt."

"Hmm . . . The Universal Store is closed today, and tomorrow I'll be at the factory. You'll have to choose your own overcoat. How much money do you have?"

Ionel Pîslari no longer seemed so hungover.

"Well, a hundred and fifty-seven rubles and fifty kopecks. Do you think that's enough?" asked Grisha Furdui, feeling a cold chill run down his spine.

"Enough and then some! Let me explain how you should choose. You've made a good decision, Grisha, but . . . we need to celebrate it!"

"Damn it! I almost forgot!" exclaimed Grisha Furdui, getting up and emptying his bag on the table, which was strewn with crumbs and shriveled potato peelings.

Ionel Pîslari cheered up. He put the jug of wine in the ramshackle refrigerator and suggested that the villager wash himself at the sink. Grisha Furdui now became fully aware of the advantages of city life. Washing in Tîrşiţa was a chore; here it was a delightful ritual.

With an emphatic gesture, Ionel Pîslari uncorked the jug and filled two dirty glasses.

"Your health!"

"And yours!"

They drained their glasses and greedily started eating the hen and the sheep's cheese.

"Hey, Vanya, you lot live in clover here! It's a big thing to have a roof over your head in the city!" said Grisha Furdui, barely containing his envy.

"Well, it's not quite like that. I toil like a workhorse all day at the factory," said Ionel Pîslari, chomping away.

"We all have to toil, but in Tîrşiţa we don't have sinks or gas cookers . . ." said the villager, heaving a sigh.

His gaze now fell on the cast-iron radiator under the windowsill.

"Does that thing give off enough heat in winter?"

"It's too damned hot! My son is always getting a headache because of it."

"I was just about to ask you where the wife and kids are . . ."

"There at my mother-in-law's. Lyuba is on holiday . . ." said Ionel Pîslari, as if talking to himself and momentarily coming round from his hangover.

After they had finished the jug and gobbled the hen, they reflected for a long time on what they should do before bedtime. Finally, they decided to liven up their existence a little: they would go to the Patria Cinema. Who knows when they would have the chance again! On the way to the cinema, they drank some lemonade, bought themselves Shipr eau de cologne, went to a clothes store, then a tavern, where, after knocking back a few mugs, they stared in puzzlement at a bizarre sign on the wall: *Alkogoli – vrag lich'nosti!*[13] All expenses were willingly paid by the man who had the money "and then some."

At the Patria, a popular Indian film was showing. Ionel Pîslari hadn't seen an Indian film since he was young, and Grisha Furdui had only been to a film projection twice in his life, at the club in the neighboring village. Well and truly drunk by now, they found it difficult to follow the plot of the film, which was constantly interrupted by heart-rending songs. The protagonists—the son of a rich malefactor and the son of a good pauper—were locked in a life-and-death struggle. Despite hostile circumstances and the omnipotence of the rich malefactor, the son of the good pauper put up a fight, always believing he would prevail. He was beaten to a pulp, but he fought on.

---

[13] Russian: "Alcohol is the foe of the personality!"

He was thrown in jail, but he fought on. His fiancée was raped, but he stubbornly fought on, as if he were a hero of the Soviet Army. Finally, he succeeded—to the great joy of his cousins—in slaying the son of the rich malefactor. The bad part was that, by terrible coincidence—his slain mortal enemy was his twin brother, who had gone missing long years before. This unexpected, disturbing ending, sent a chill through Grisha Fudui's heart. Next to him, resting her chin on her hands, a pensioner was weeping softly. Even the former cinephile Ionel Pîslari felt harrowed.

They returned to the hostel as night fell, they drank more beer, they played Belote, they nattered, and they fell asleep, weary, liberated from routine obligations and family compromises.

WRITER I.C.: *The Party slogan about liqui-dating the differences between village and town, between physical and intellectual labor, has become a visible reality in our everyday lives. For centuries, the bourgeois parties, hunting the peas-ant vote at elections, called the peasantry the sole of the nation's opanak. The great renewal brought by the rays of the October Revolution has erased this demagogic and insulting term. With the disappear-ance of the opanak has come the disappearance of illiteracy, backwardness and poverty. Villages built*

on new foundations go hand in hand with net-
works of asphalted roads, electricity pylons, which
illumine every house and every mind. Today, to
say that television, radio, natural gas, secondary
school, culture clubs, commercial centers, commu-
nal services, hospitals, and telephone networks are
goods with which villagers are familiar is to take
note of a highly ordinary truth. Working condi-
tions are changing, people's psychology is changing.
It is our duty to mirror this spiritual growth, to
capture convincingly man's inner world.

The country road was long and—the icing on the
cake—there was not a cart in sight. Grisha Furdui
walked slowly, hunched with bitterness more than
because of the blazing sun. He was thinking of the
miraculous city. Everything had captivated him so
intensely, everything had been so perfect there, that
it no longer really mattered that he had squandered
the money he ought to have spent on the overcoat he
desired. There were so many things he had never even
known about, never wondered about. How could he
have been so blind? There were light years between
the world of Ionel Pîslari and his own rustic world
peopled by the slaves of routine. How could the peasants of Tîrșița live like sleepwalkers? How could they

waste their time on such insignificant things? Some of them were so busy that for days at a time they did not so much as exchange two words with their neighbors, despite getting up at the crack of dawn. Nothing but work and more work!

And what was his work in that place? He mucked out the dung from the cow sheds! And how did he do it? With a shovel and a pitchfork. Whereas at other farms they had special machinery, transporters with scrapers. Instead of mucking out just three or four times a day, he had to toil like an idiot from dawn till dusk! An unpleasant shudder went down his spine.

He would have to travel to the city once a week till he found a permanent job there. He would have to fight like the son of the good pauper in the Indian film. In the end, not even Ionel Pîslaru spoke fluent Russian and he hadn't had a residence permit when he discovered the city.

At the bottom of the lane flanked by ramshackle houses was his own hovel. He entered the yard, looking around him, disconcerted. Everything looked grey, empty, desolate. Everything got on his nerves here: the strident squawking of an old hen, which he couldn't bear to slaughter, the oinking of a hungry pig, the rachitic, dirty, barefoot children. A strange sensation of muffled fear took hold of him. His withered, frigid wife appeared, springing as if from the earth, and started pleading with him to fix a door that had come off its hinges.

Grisha Furdui spat bitterly. Was it really worth the effort?

"To hell with the fucking door, you stupid woman! Have you any idea what a life Vanya Pîslari lives?"

The Courtyard

ALTHOUGH IT WAS a Saturday, Iulian had been at home alone since early that morning. Bitterly, his father had left for the factory, as if going off to war. His mother had taken the bus to Străşeni to sell her knitted mohair sweaters at the flea market. The wages of laborer Vladimir Vladimirovich and Olga Leonovna did not stretch to the instalments on the hire-purchase wardrobe and sofa.

It was as if time had stood still.

Iulian was bored. He had already studied the map of the world to the point of satiety, observing yet again that for the time being the territories controlled by the imperialists were vaster than the Soviet Union. He didn't even feel like reading science-fiction novels. He would have gone outside, but the courtyard had become a perilous area ever since Baranov and Zuckerman caught him and almost gave him a thrashing the previous week. He had to be cautious.

The incident played back before his mind's eye.

Although Larik Schreibman, his best friend, had warned him that Zuckerman had been after him for quite some time, Iulian had blithely ignored the danger. They had caught up with him behind the building, in the middle of the day, and, without wasting time, they had dragged him to the hedge, out of the sight of other tenants' prying eyes. Their faces were impenetrable. Iulian took a punch to the chin, which felled him. He lay with his knees raised to his chin, to protect his genitals from the furious onslaught of their training shoes.

"*Za chto?*"[14] he managed to shout before bursting into tears.

"*Khuilo! Byk konchenyy, mul, peasant, ovtsa tuporylaya . . .*"[15] growled Baranov.

A roar from the decrepit war veteran, who appeared out of the blue, caused them to freeze: "*Yob vashu mat', podonki! On tozhe sovetskiy chelovek!*"[16]

Aleksey Petrovich—whom Iulian glimpsed as if through a haze—brandished his feeble fist at the bullies, hurrying up to them. The medals of the defender

---

[14] Russian: "What for?"

[15] Russian: "Dickhead! Knackered ox, mule . . . dumb sheep."

[16] Russian: "Fuck your mother! Scum! He's a Soviet citizen too!"

of Stalingrad and veteran of the Jassy-Kishinev operation jingled menacingly. He always wore them, regard-
less of whether he was at a parade or queuing at the
food store. Taking fright, Baranov and Zuckerman
ran away . . .

It was actually in the nature of things that Aleksey
Petrovich should rescue him. At least once a week,
his father and the veteran stuffed their bellies and
talked their jaws off at the canteen three minutes from
their building. The canteen had made them eternal
bosom buddies. His mother thought that Vladimir
Vladimirovich was pouring money down the drain
and risked becoming an alcoholic. She would reel
off a list of all their acquaintances who had ended up
being taken to hospital in an alcoholic coma. She told
him he would die prematurely and they wouldn't have
enough money to bury him. There were quarrels. His
father would yell that he toiled till he was fit to drop,
that he was like a workhorse, that he could no longer
abide her daily nagging, and that he therefore had
the right to at least a tot of vodka. His mother took
pills for headaches. She chided him for failing to get
into university and held up as an example somebody
called Pogreban—a complete chucklehead—who had
two apartments, a Zhiguli car, a garage, and a dacha,
and who holidayed in resorts in the Caucasus. With
his head bowed, Iulian would listed to these quarrels,

which had become a permanent fixture of his child-hood. Most of the time he took his mother's side, but on occasion he would also grant that his father was right, especially when he remembered Stakhanov. His father worked like Stakhanov, he was industrious, and Iulian couldn't understand why his mother didn't have enough money.

One evening, when the quarrel seemed to be never-ending, Iulian ran out of the apartment, slamming the door behind him, and forgetting all about his mother's ban on him leaving the house after nightfall. In the evening, long-haired hooligans disturbed the peace in the courtyard, drinking beer, singing along to a guitar, playing poker, and swearing their heads off. Some of them arrived on rumbling motorcycles, to the chronic exasperation of the tenants. In the beginning, the hooligans had liked to sit on the benches in front of Iulian's building. The tenants would come out onto their balconies to demand they keep it down.

"*Zakroy yebalo, chuchelo!*"[17] the hooligans would yell, blatantly ignoring the tenants' warnings. The tenants then called the police. The hooligans would disperse, only to reappear the next evening, more defi-ant and raucous than before. At the suggestion of Aleksey Petrovich and despite the opposition of the

---

[17] Russian: "Shut your fuck-hole, scarecrow!"

old biddies, who liked to prattle there, the revolted tenants took axes to all the benches. The long-haired motorcyclists withdrew to the nearby sports field and the warring parties made a truce . . .

That evening, Iulian ran out of the apartment and, completely forgetting about the hooligans, went to the sports field. Darkness had already fallen. A hoarse voice, accompanied by a guitar, stopped him in his tracks.

> *Gop-stop! My podoshli iz za ugla!*
> *Gop-stop! Ty mnogo na sebya vzyala . . .*[18]

He expected to be beaten up. But surprisingly, the hooligans turned out to be friendly. They suggested he drink a beer. He timidly declined. A burly lad, in whose arms reclined a nubile young thing in a mini-skirt, offered him a cigarette. He declined once more. He asked them to speak Moldavian, at which they laughed at him, gave him a condom and advised him to be gallant with the girls.

The condom was like an oily balloon.

Fear had been at his back ever since the day when Baranov and Zuckerman had caught him. To reveal to his parents what had befallen him would have meant cutting the branch from under himself. Snitches

---

[18] Russian: "Hop-hop! I come around the corner! / Hop-hop! You've grabbed a lot for yourself!" (Lines from a song popular with the black marketeers who got rich in the Brezhnev period.)

were savagely punished in the courtyard; everybody pointed the finger at them. A lad who failed to seal his lips went from the frying pan into the fire. They would make him drink fetid water from the puddles by the garbage cans. The most frightening thing that could happen would be for Aleksey Petrovich to tell his father everything and then for him to be unfairly branded a snitch. He was weedy and quite cowardly. His cheeks burned for shame when the girls in his class or from the courtyard casually remarked that he was nothing but skin and bones and advised him to eat more. One of the laws of the Pioneers of the Soviet Union dictated that a pioneer "always courageously stands up for the truth." He did not even have the courage to sneak up behind his enemies and throw a rock at them. Would he have been able to defend the homeland with a gun in his hand? Would he have been able to kill a German general, like Lyonya Golikov? Would he have been able to charge into a hopeless battle against the Nazis, like Pioneer Marat Kazey, and kill ten fascists? Such rhetorical questions depressed him. A badge inscribed R.L.D. (Ready for Labor and Defense), as proudly worn by the muscular Baranov, seemed an impossible goal.

It was half past three in the afternoon. His parents had still not come back. He turned on the television, having first fetched a bottle of milk and a loaf of bread from the kitchen. One of the joys of his childhood was to drink milk and eat bread while watching the television. *Po Zayavkam Rabotnikov Zhivotnovodstva*[19] was one of his favorite programs, but only because it was always followed by a feature film. The heroine of that day's episode was Stakhanovite cow-milker Frăsîna Paierele from the Crişcăuţi village farm.

> *. . . Outside, day is barely breaking. Crişcăuţi collective farm is still sleeping, immersed in perfect silence. Light twinkles in the windows of only a few houses. We hear the creak of doors. Voices come from the almost deserted lanes. It is the milkers from Frăsîna Paierele's team, who are hurrying to the farm. They are the first to start work. How numerous are the responsibilities of a milker! She must curry and water the cows, milk them three times a day, wash them, and massage their udders. Every one of these things requires great skill: you have to know the temperament of every cow and her appetite. For every cow has her quirks . . .*

Iulian knew what was eating them. Baranov and Zuckerman hated him because they thought him a *byk*. Larik Schreibman had explained it to him in

---

painstaking detail. A *byk* was somebody who looked as if he had been raised in the woods, he was swarthy, tanned, stupid, a peasant, ignorant, coarse, he dressed tastelessly and spoke poor Russian. His daily occupations were hoeing, harvesting, milking.

"Don't worry about it!" said Larik, placing a reassuring hand on Iulian's shoulder. "If you were a *byk*, I wouldn't be your friend. You speak Russian as well as I do, you're the best ping-pong player in the courtyard, you're a good footballer, you're intelligent, you wear jeans, not homespun trousers. Do you know why a *byk* pickles vegetables in a barrel? Because his head won't fit in a jar!"

Larik laughed heartily. Iulian's laughter was more subdued: he remembered seeing a pickle barrel in the cellar of his Aunt Talyusya in Tătărăuca Veche.

Over the course of thousands of years, milking has been a manual operation: sitting on a stool or kneeling, the woman milked the cow. After milking, her hands would smart as if she had carried endless burdens. Today, the milkers have modern machinery at their disposal, automatic feeding and watering equipment, electrical milking devices. At some farms, milking is carried out using portable machines, at others, fixed milking installations are employed.

"The truth is that my ma was born in a village . . ." confessed Iulian, lowering his eyes.

"She can't be a *bykovka* if she has a son like you! Baranov and Zuckerman are idiots. The world is full of *byki*, and they're just picking on a normal person."

A weight was lifted from Iulian's soul.

. . . The cows enter the milking room one by one, they take their places in front of the mangers. The milkers deftly attach the milking apparatuses to the teats and turn them on. While the cows have their breakfast, lunch or supper, the milk flows through the tubes to the storage tanks.

Larik Schreibman was his best friend. They were neighbors; they lived on the same floor. *Tyotya* Haya, Larik's grandmother, often gave Iulian candies and crumbly biscuits, which you couldn't find in the stores or markets, and patted him on the head. She would sometimes come to Iulian's house and talk for a long time with his mother in the tiny kitchen where the refrigerator rumbled like a tractor. It was astonishing how *tyotya* Haya could speak perfect Moldavian. Her accent was both pleasant and unusual. But *tyotya* Haya spoke Moldavian only to Iulian's mother in the kitchen. How and why had she learned Moldavian? Iulian had once overheard, despite the refrigerator drowning out the conversation, *tyotya* Haya telling his mother that she would like to leave the Soviet Union. The thought that his friend might end up a slave of the imperialists horrified Iulian. Larik reassured him that he wasn't going anywhere. When the Czechoslovak fun fair came to town and Iulian was filled with despair because his parents couldn't give him any money to go, *tyotya* Haya used to find a few rubles to make the two lads happy. They would buy Pedro chewing gum and, with shudders of fascination, enter the "chamber of horrors." Iulian didn't have a bicycle. But that was no problem, because Larik had an Orlyonok. Iulian's mother bought him a pullover or training shoes only once in a blue moon. Well, for his birthday, Larik bought him a magnificent waterproof jacket. True, Iulian did not go to the Crimea every summer, instead going to Koblevo, albeit seldom; true, he lived in a two-room apartment, rather than a spacious three-room apartment with a hall, but that didn't matter. He remembered his astonishment on discovering the poster of Jimmy Carter in Larik's bedroom. The chief of the imperialists was on horseback and wearing a cowboy hat.

"You've got to admit that his cowboy hat is nicer than Leonid Ilyich's medals," said Larik, in his defense.

. . . Every milker has thirty, fifty and sometimes even more cows in her care. Every year, champion milker Frăsîna Paierele attends the Exhibition of Soviet National Economic Achievements in Moscow, where she deftly demonstrates her triumphs of labor. The skill of Frăsîna Paierele is highly appreciated; she has been awarded the title of Hero of Socialist Labor.

Iulian's eyes bulged. He all but choked on his bread and milk. Frăsîna Paierele looked exactly like a *bykovka*. Could a *bykovka* really be a Hero of Socialist Labor?

The telephone buzzed. It was Larik.

"Iulik, are you a man? We've got to go and teach a *byk* from the next building some respect. He's putting on airs . . . Are you with us?"

The Death Announcement

PAVEL FYODOROVICH KAVRIG, deputy to the head of the ideology section of the City Party Committee awoke with a pleasant feeling of languor and, in keeping with his longstanding habit, he lingered in bed, stretching, savoring the matutinal tranquility of another Sunday. Lately, even though his weekday schedule was far from busy, Pavel Fyodorovich had looked forward to the weekend, to the days when he slowed down, and when his professional obligations and assignments—they were difficult, there was no denying it—ceased to demand his attention.

From time to time, a breath of air coming through the open window caused the blue curtains to undulate and gave Pavel Fyodorovich the impression that he was looking at the azure surface of a calm sea. He yawned and stretched once more. An intermittent dull clinking sound confirmed that his wife Lyusya was doing her duty: she was making him a breakfast rich in vitamins. Pavel Fyodorovich licked his lips and tried to sit up in bed. It was not as easy as it seemed. He had to make a repeated effort, and not without a trace of regret, to relinquish his sweet, all-encompassing lassitude.

He found his slippers, put on his dressing gown, took his Dutch cigarette case from the bedside table on which sat a vase of pleasantly smelling flowers, and went out onto the balcony. He lit an expensive cigarette, took a deep drag, and ran his fingers through his greying hair. Pushkin Park, gilded by the rays of the rising sun, slumbered in perfect silence. The only sounds were a sprinkler humming in the distance and the mumbling of a divorced street sweeper who was in the habit of tippling on the job at the break of day.

"Pavlush-a-a! Breakfast's ready!" resounded the triumphal voice of his wife from the kitchen, providing further confirmation of the fact that his life was taking its customary course. He tossed his cigarette butt off the balcony (let the street sweeper do her job!) and headed for the bathroom, where he continued his routine. He brushed his healthy set of teeth, examined them with satisfaction in the mirror, and then seated himself on the toilet, humming a merry tune:

A nam vsyo ravno![20] He then casually strolled into the spacious dining room and seated himself at the head of the table. Lyusya had already laid the table and brought in the pot-bellied samovar.

She was a nondescript, middle-aged woman, who for years and years had tried in vain—by means of excessive make-up and garish clothes—to keep up with the glamorous wives of the Party bigwigs. There had been a time when Pavel Fyodorovich had encouraged her in her unshakeable determination to rise to the required level, buying her all kinds of frocks, shoes, and exotic cosmetics on his trips abroad. But after a time, his wife's appearance ceased to interest Pavel Fyodorovich, except on those days when he had to appear with her in society. On such days, Pavel Fyodorovich would be surprised to discover that his wife looked old before her time, and Lyusya would timidly scold him for not giving her enough pocket money, even to buy herself local clothes.

"Let's see what's for breakfast today!" exclaimed Pavel Fyodorovich, running his eyes over the fruit salad, pastrami, sausages, sheep's cheese, and olives on the table. It was a ritual exclamation, which for Lyusya had only one meaning: her husband was satisfied and was praising her. And indeed, Pavel Fyodorovich

---

[20] Russian: "It's all the same to us!"

straightaway started to gobble up his breakfast, blinking his eyes in pleasure after every mouthful.

"Pavlusha, let's go to the Chekhov Theatre this evening. Panteleyevna told me it's the premiere of a very interesting tragedy with characters from the Middle Ages!" said Lyusya, pouring hot water from the samovar into the teacups.

Panteleyevna was the wife of a bigwig from the Soviet of Ministers, a man whose second job was whoring. His wife had had a nasty shock when she happened to walk in on her husband as he frenziedly rode a secretary on the desk in an office of one of the most important institutions of the republic. But it was not the betrayal in itself that horrified Panteleyevna so much as the secondary details that caught her eye as she stepped through the door of the office: the secretary's ripped knickers, the passion of her ageing and seemingly apathetic husband, and above all the age of her rival, who was definitely no younger than fifty. Much later, remembering that turning point, which had poisoned her entire life, she realized that she had lost sight of an even more repulsive fact: the disgusting pair had not even bothered to lock the door. It was around that time that Panteleyevna, who did not deign to file for divorce, felt a keen interest in the theatre for the first time in her life, and in tragedies in particular, a genre all too rare and out of keeping with the spirit of the age. She began to go to the theatre and in the end passed on her passion to her friend Lyusya, much to the annoyance of Pavel Fyodorovich, who foresaw danger in his wife's predilection for plays with tragic endings. There wouldn't have been any cause for concern if Lyusya had stuck to the usual tragedies, in which the Heroes of the Great War to Defend the Homeland were villainously slain by Hitler's henchmen, but she was mad about the macabre tragedies penned by the ancients and obscure mediaeval writers—who knows why anybody staged them—which concerned family conflicts, betrayals, adultery, betrayals, and bloody vengeance. Pavel Fyodorovich, on the other hand, liked to watch films at the cinema, especially zany comedies, and couldn't comprehend why a happy woman like Lyusya sought out mediaeval tragedies in the company of a woman whose suffering was incurable. Was it a good thing that Lyusya consorted with the slighted wife of a womanizing Party bigwig?

"That's a good one! The Middle Ages again!" said Pavel Fyodorovich, giving his partner in life a reproving look. His silver fork, on which was impaled a plump olive, paused in mid-air. "What have we got to do with the Middle Ages? What the hell has got into you? I'm not surprised that Pantaleyevna is so keen on that tear-jerking stuff, but what's wrong with you? I'm going to ban that nutcase from coming to our house!"

"Oh dear, Pavlusha! You're getting all annoyed over nothing. You don't know what you're talking about. If you came with me just once, you'd see that the mediaeval characters are so authentic that you'd think they were contemporary people in disguise. And how is Pantaleyevna to blame if her husband cheated on her? You know very well she's a decent sort. I'm begging you, Pavlusha, don't say anything to her, she's very unhappy . . ." said Lyusya, aggrieved.

"What the hell!" Pavel Fyodorovich suddenly exclaimed, slapping his forehead. With slight disappointment, he had suddenly remembered that he was meant to go to a party being thrown by a bigwig at a dacha in Condriţa. Not that he wouldn't have liked to eat red wine-drizzled skewered meat or enjoyed the whoops of the musicians, but he wanted to be able to relax at least on a Sunday, to forget about having to be cautious, not to be fearful lest he say the wrong thing. But he had no choice.

"No question of my going to the theatre! I have to be in Condriţa this evening. That old fox Pyotr Kirillovich would notice if I weren't there. Are you coming with me?"

"Pavlusha, I'd like to go to the premiere if it's all the same to you . . ."

The good mood he had been in when he woke up began to desert Pavel Fyodorovich.

"Do whatever you like . . ." he said in a grumpy voice, getting up from the table and trying to remember which of the cognacs in his collection it was that Pyotr Kirillovich liked the best. At bigwig parties it wasn't recommended to arrive empty-handed.

Right then a heavily made-up, blasé blonde entered the dining room, undulating her lithe body: Pavel Fyodorovich's only daughter. A third-year student at the Polytechnic Institute, she was bored to death of her course, which she deemed pointless. Only the prestige and eloquence of Pavel Fyodorovich had allayed the danger of her being expelled. The fact that the father needed his daughter's university degree more than she did only appeared to be a paradox: Marina could take advantage of her father's social status in every situation, whereas with his status Pavel Fyodorovich's could not afford to have a daughter who had been expelled from university.

Wearing jeans and a clinging white lace blouse that showed off her ample bosom, Marina sat down at the table, tossed an olive in her mouth, chewed slowly, spat out the stone, put on a sly face, and bluntly stated: "*Papanya*, we're getting married . . ."

"Who's *we*?" asked Pavel Fyodorovich, raising his eyebrows in surprise. He could sense an unpleasant unease growing within him.

"Garik Popov and me! He's the cousin of one of

the girls in my group. We're going to get married, *Papanya!*"

"What's that? Are you joking?"

"No way, *Papanya*. I couldn't be more serious. I want you to meet Garik. He's coming here next Sunday."

Marina seemed very self-assured.

"He's coming here . . ." repeated Pavel Fyodorovich in perplexity.

A tomb-like silence descended. Although usually he displayed perfect self-control, it took a few moments for him to recover and suppress his unease.

"Have you known each other long?" asked Pavel Fyodorovich in a faint voice.

"Almost a year," said Marina with a smile, as if she considered the period of time irrelevant.

The annoying sense of unease once more stole into Pavel Fyodorovich's soul.

"A year? How come I didn't know anything about it? What about university? What are you going to do about university?" he asked, hoarse with annoyance.

Obviously, like any father, Pavel Fyodorovich had often imagined his daughter's wedding, but he shared the belief widespread among Party bigwigs that the matrimonial course of the progeny must be under the control of the progenitor. On the other hand, his daughter's blasé attitude and her defiant nature had always made him fear that he would be confronted with a fait accompli. And this is what had indeed happened. He could not take his eyes off his daughter. He would have liked her to laugh loudly and tell him it was all a joke, and he would have admitted, with relief, that a very good joke it was too. But he sensed she was serious. At one point, he thought Marina cast her mother a complicit glance. An unpleasant, tardy realization flashed through his mind: his daughter was talking only to him, consequently Lyusya knew everything. A suspicion arose in his mind, which prompted him to be drastic, to get to the bottom of it immediately. Why had his wife and daughter concealed a fact of which, under normal circumstances, he ought to have been apprised? Had Marina and this Garik slept together by any chance? Had this individual dishonored his daughter? Although that was hardly likely, since Marina was far from looking like a victim. Was she . . . pregnant?

He felt his legs giving way beneath him.

It was highly possible that Garik might be a mere adventurer, a pauper out for material gain. Since she was so keen on tragedies, how come Lyusya didn't understand the danger that stalked them? It all seemed incomprehensible to him. He remembered grandmother Frăsîna, who, whenever she saw him in good spirits, used to say that a man was heading for a fall when life couldn't seem better.

Marina tossed another olive in her mouth. She seemed disappointed at her father's reaction. Stiffly, Pavel Fyodorovich turned to his wife: "What the hell is going on? One thinks about nothing but the theatre, and the other wants to get married before she finishes university. What the hell are the two of you up to? Did you both make a plot to ruin my good mood first thing in the morning?"

Pavel Fyodorovich's voice was indignant and Lyusya realized that things were turning nasty. She hastened to reassure her husband: "Calm down, Pavlusha. Everything is all right. Garik is a nice boy, and his father has a *high-ranking position*! We didn't tell you because . . . we didn't know how to . . . But it would be a good thing if you met Garik . . ."

"You didn't know how to! But you know how to hatch plots! Who am I supposed to be in this house? Am I nothing? I don't want to hear anything more about this Garik! It isn't Garik who's the problem, the problem is that I've pussyfooted around you both for too long!"

Pavel Fyodorovich stalked out of the dining room tense with rage, despite the fact that Garik's father had a "high-ranking position."

He went straight to his office and sinking into a Sobakevich-style armchair, reflected at length on the unwanted turn of events. Finally, his annoyance abated somewhat, he regretted that he had lost his temper before even meeting that Garik, and he even recovered his equanimity, imagining what it would be like to have a son-in-law with such a powerful father. He wanted to know what position Garik's father held. Might he have been making a lot of fuss about nothing?

Reinvigorated, he went to the solid-oak cupboard, opened the minibar, and carefully examined his valuable collection. Crowded there were some thirty bottles brought back from foreign trips, bathed in the faint, flickering glow of a little red light bulb. He took out a bottle of Cuban rum, stood pensive for a few seconds, heaved a deep sigh, and put it back. He had no choice. The finicky Pyotr Kirillovich liked only Napoleon brandy. He would have to part with his last bottle of brandy, for which he had paid, in a shop in Moscow, no less than thirty rubles: half the salary of a nursery school teacher.

Since he had time aplenty before the Volga arrived to take him to Condriţa, he dozed through a comedy film on television, went to the living room and attenuated something of his daughter's apathy by saying he would make a final decision after meeting Garik. He asked his wife what was for lunch and then left the apartment to go for a walk in the park.

On the landing, leaning on the bannister of the stairs, an octogenarian wreck was catching his breath.

"How are things going, Pavel? Working hard?" asked the retired politruk with evident curiosity.

Pavel Fyodorovich always tried to avoid him, although not because he had a croaking voice and disconcertingly steady gaze. The reason was different: the veteran's only means of bracketing off the monotony of his days was to intercept people on the stairs and talk their ears off.

"Yes, I'm working hard, Boris Borisovich, working hard. What else can I do?" said Pavel Fyodorovich, simulating friendliness and thinking how to rid himself of the irritating old man more quickly.

The retired politruk instantly put on a vague smile: "That's the way, Pavel! Strike while the iron is hot! Where would we be if we didn't have hard work or, more accurately, if we didn't work for the benefit of society? Where would we be if we didn't have well-paid work? I was young like you once, Pavel, I worked hard for the benefit of the Army, I was wounded at Stalingrad, it wasn't easy for me and here I am, starting to wonder: *to what end?* It's painful, Pavel, to reach old age and discover that to some people my hard work wasn't worth so much as a withered onion! I'm the fifth wheel on the cart now! *But it's a good thing that your generation isn't threatened by such a danger . . .*"

He uttered the last sentence in a malicious, mocking tone, which threw Pavel Fyodorovich slightly off balance.

"What's the matter, Boris Borisovich?" he asked, trying to conceal his annoyance. He had no inclination to be the old man's confidant. But Boris Borisovich, the man who had so often talked his ears off, merely made a weary gesture and continued to climb the stairs, clinging to the bannister.

"The *starik*[21] is off his rocker! Or maybe one of the younger bigwigs has offended him? Let's say that's what happened. But why has he got it in for *me*? Let's say there are people who don't pay any attention to him. But he's got a big pension, a three-room apartment in the centre of town, the state pays his bills, he gets a yearly holiday in Sergeyevka. What the hell more does the old codger want?" wondered Pavel Fyodorovich indignantly.

The good part was that he'd got rid of him far more quickly than he'd anticipated.

In the park, he sat down on a bench near the bust of Pushkin and snoozed for a little, soothed by the gentle rays of the sun. Children were chasing each other around the fountain, bumping into the people out and about. A few pensioners were walking their dogs, which urinated against the trunks of the trees.

---

[21] Russian: "Old codger."

"How wonderful it is to be left in peace" thought Pavel Fyodorovich.

After a while, he looked at his watch, stood up, and went to the newspaper stand by the bus stop. He bought his favorite papers—*Sovetsky Sport, Pravda*, and *Moldova Socialistă*—and went home. From his daughter's room came loud music, an infernal racket. Lyusya was busy preparing a copious lunch in the kitchen. All smiles, he asked her what position Garik's father had. She said it was a surprise; he would find out the next Sunday.

"Hmm, we'll see . . ." said Pavel Fyodorovich and retired to his office to read the papers.

Sovetsky Sport examined the reasons for the constant victories of the Soviet hockey team and the causes of the no less constant defeats of the Soviet football team. An idea of bourgeois origin was demolished, namely that the Soviet Union was a northern country, and it was strongly asserted that unlike the lazy, defeatist footballers, the hockey players were "always increasing their theoretical-ideological level and perfecting their skill." "Oh, come off it!" said Pavel Fyodorovich with a smile. *Pravda* recounted that comrade Mengistu Haile Mariam—the leader of the Ethiopian revolution and the hope of the African continent—had arrived in Moscow. A photograph on the first page captured the passionate embrace of

comrades L.I. Brezhnev and M.H. Mariam. Pavel
Fyodorovich skimmed the pages of *Pravda*, which
unmasked the machinations of global imperial-
ism, and then unfolded *Moldova Socialistă*. Zealous
Moldavian agriculturalists were working day and
night to meet the targets of the new five-year plan
before schedule. A writer of the people had visited
Tîrșița cow farm. The reporter said that literature
"thereby strengthens its ties with the life of the people
and with truthfulness, inspiration and consummate
writerly skill reflects the socialist reality."

Tucked away in the bottom right-hand corner
of the last page were a few death announcements.
Although he didn't like such funereal stuff, he always
read the announcements, filled with a vague unease.
A Hero of Socialist Labor, a leading agronomist, a
surgeon . . . All of a sudden, a surname struck him,
and Pavel Fyodorovich experienced a sensation like
that of a cold draught. He abruptly crumpled up the
newspaper, as if to throw it away, but then stopped
himself. He sat for a few moments staring into space.
He then unfolded the newspaper with a shiver. He
could not believe his eyes. The bottommost rectangle
contained the following text:

> *Her colleagues and friends express*
> *their sincere condolences*
> *to comrade Ion Puică of the Institute of*
> *Physics*
> *of the Academy of Sciences of the S.S.R.M.*
> *on the decease of his wife*
> ***Elena Lungu.***
> *We will not forget her.*

Komsomol leader Pavel Kavrig had met Lenuța Lungu in the summer of 1958, when he was getting ready to take part in the virgin lands campaign on the Kazakh steppe. With a few of his pals, he had gone to the dances held in a public garden. He had danced with all the attractive girls before he happened to notice her, during a break between the songs played by the brass band. She was not a particularly beautiful girl and the dashing young men took no notice of her, preferring her dolled-up, languorous, mouthy friends. But the Komsomol leader was instantly conquered by the unfamiliar girl's vaguely bashful air; he was astonished by the delicacy of her gestures. He extricated himself from the impatient, fancily dressed floozy who kept insisting he dance with her, strode straight up to the plain girl and, without wasting time, engaged her in conversation, employing all his Komsomol skills of persuasion. They excitedly discussed things of no importance, forgetting all about his jaunty pals and her dolled-up girlfriends. Lenuța Lungu was a student at the Pedagogical Institute and she had a gifted turn of speech that Pavel Kavrig had never before encountered and which the girl's vaguely bashful air made utterly charming. He walked her home. Lenuța Lungu lived with her widowed mother in an old house that was crooked but not lacking in elegance, at the edge of Buiucani. By the gate, he drew her to him and she did not put up much resistance.

"I'm not looking for just a fling . . ." she whispered, quivering.

She then fell into his arms.

The next day, Pavel Kavrig met Lenuța's mother, who was left astounded: she had seen the unmistakable face of the Komsomol wunderkind on the first page of a major newspaper. The devoted mother hastened to laid the table, overwhelmed by her daughter's incredible good fortune. That day, Pavel Kavrig went home at nightfall, his belly bursting. On the third day, the two youngsters retired to Lenuța's room and, taking advantage of the widow's diminished perspicuity, made love too passionately and too hastily. The affair lasted a week, after which Pavel Kavrig departed at the head of a band of zealous Komsomolists to set records on the Kazakh steppe. Four months later, he returned to Kishinev for a few days. The bearded, flustered Pavel Kavrig rushed to see his girlfriend. Lenuța's face was drawn and she had put on weight. She was with child and thinking about marriage. Horrified, the Komsomol leader had not been expecting such a turn of events. Although he was sure the child was his, he furiously demanded proof her fidelity in his absence. Lenuța Lungu had never been subjected to such a painful insult. She burst into tears. Pavel Kavrig stormed out of the house and never saw her again.

One of her dolled-up friends, whom Pavel Fyodorovich bumped into many years later, recognizing her only with difficulty, told him that Lenuța had had a backstreet abortion and survived only by a miracle.

"She married a physicist without any money . . ." the former dolled-up girlfriend told him, full of sympathy.

Stricken, Pavel Fyodorovich studied the death announcement for a few long minutes. He tried to explain to himself why, after so many years, Lenuța's death troubled him so greatly. He had all but forgotten her, he had had no idea what life she had led, he had led his own life and it was as if he were a wholly

contented man. True, she had appeared to him a couple of times in his dreams: she would be holding a child
in her arms and she would timidly scold him, while
he, overwhelmed by her reproach, instantly accepted
the entire blame, the full shame of it. He had woken
in a sweat. But what were two or three troubled nights
compared with the calm of twenty years of marriage.
A drop in the ocean. Nonetheless, this conclusion did
not console him.

He didn't want to go to the bigwigs' party. He
opened the bottle of brandy intended for Pyotr
Kirillovich, took a swig, and tried to put his thoughts
in order. It was true that since the distant day when
he found out she was pregnant he had dreamed her
just three times, but an important detail, which had
escaped him, was that those tormented nights had all
been recently. Was the thought that death can snatch
away the people you know at any moment really be the
reason for the unease that now gripped his soul? Not
at all. Pavel Fyodorovich felt guilty and probably for
the last twenty years he had hidden away his guilt in
the deepest recesses of his soul. It had attenuated the
possibility of his being forgiven. He rested his chin on
his hands and closed his eyes. Now the woman who
had to forgive him no longer existed. He sank back in
the armchair with a groan. He wondered why Lenuţa
had left him alone—she could easily have caused him

problems—and the feeling of guilt became unbearable. And the thudding music from his daughter's
room was also becoming unbearable.

"Turn that music down!" yelled Pavel Fyodorovich,
poking his head out of the door of his office. His
shaky voice would not have had any effect on Marina
had Pavel Fyodorovich not agreed to Garik's visit.

Had he loved her? He didn't know, because he
couldn't really say what the word *love* meant. He had
never uttered the word and he smiled sarcastically or
snorted whenever he heard other people say it. Pavel
Fyodorovich was a firm believer in pragmatism. But
he now realized—without having made a thorough
examination of his conscience—that for the last week
he had been experiencing a profound feeling such as
he had never encountered in the last twenty years.
Lenuţa had been the one who had aroused in him a
deep sensuality. He had married Lyusya from conve-
nience: she was the daughter of an influential bigwig,
and without her help he wouldn't have been able to
climb the ladder. She was a good woman, an industrious housewife; he had nothing to complain about on
that score. It would be their silver wedding before he
knew it. But even so . . . hadn't the apathy of self-con-
tentment stolen into their lives? It was as if something
wasn't quite right . . . For example, the fact that sometimes they didn't have anything to say to each other.

For hours on end, they would watch the television in silence, each thinking their own thoughts. Ultimately, what kept them together other than their daughter and the material belongings they had accumulated?

Over lunch, Pavel Fyodorovich told his wife that he was very tired and didn't want to go to the party any more.

"What's wrong, Pavel Fyodorovich?" Lyusya asked, alarmed by the fact that her husband wasn't feeling himself again.

"Does there have to be anything wrong if I want to be left in peace?" I'm tired, that's all! That's what's wrong!" growled Pavel Fyodorovich and shut himself away in his office.

That evening, after Lyusya and Panteleyevna went out to the theatre, and Marina went off to a birthday party, Pavel Fyodorovich went out for a long aimless walk. He came back late and rather than going to bed, he slumped down on the armchair in his office. He finally fell asleep, still trying to prove to himself that he wasn't afraid to confront the past. He awoke at dawn, in the toils of a bad dream. A hideous embryo, with a large head and bulging eyes, stretched its limbs toward him and cried: You killed me, Father! The embryo's feeble gaze harrowed him, made him feel all of a sudden terribly alone.

After breakfast, he put on his shirt with the nacre

buttons, adjusted the knot of his tie, put on his East German jacket, sprayed himself with cologne, and left the spacious four-room apartment. The silver Volga was waiting for him by the entrance. The Party City Committee was just a stone's throw away, but it was not fitting that a bigwig should walk.

"You look out of sorts, Pavel. You weren't at the party. Pyotr Kirillovich was expecting you. What's wrong?" his boss asked him, looking him up and down.

"I'm exhausted, Valeri Nikolayevich. I need a holiday . . ." muttered Pavel Fyodorovich.

"Hmm . . . You were all right on Friday. Admit it, it was some young floozy who exhausted you!"

Valeri Nikolayevich laughed heartily, but on seeing that his deputy was completely down in the mouth, he became serious once more.

"Very well! I'll give you two weeks. I'll expect you to be fit, healthy and in a good mood when you get back!"

In his office, Pavel Fyodorovich made a few telephone calls and found out the address of assistant scientist Ion Puică. He hurried downstairs to the waiting Volga, slammed the door shut, and told his driver where he wanted to go.

It was a drab apartment building without balconies, built in the 1950s. On patches of waste ground heaps of garbage were rotting. Pavel Fyodorovich paused in front of the entrance, trying to quell his unease. Two old women were sitting on a bench alongside, staring at him, whispering. They gave the impression that they had nothing better to do than talk about whoever entered their field of vision. The letterboxes inside the entrance had been vandalized by the hordes of feral children. He went up to the fifth floor, hesitated on the landing for a few moments, then approached a door with peeling paint and timidly pressed the doorbell. There was no sound. He pressed the button again. Profound silence. He was about to leave when finally he heard a muffled noise.

A solidly built man with a pale, haggard face and bloodshot eyes opened the door.

"Are you Ion Puică? I read the death announcement in the paper . . . I wanted to pay my respects . . ." stammered Pavel Fyodorovich, obviously made uncomfortable by the man's unflinching stare.

"Come in . . ." said the physicist in a surly voice, stepping to one side.

The air in the dark apartment was damp, moldy. In the main room, Pavel Fyodorovich was brought up short by a sharp reek: on the table was a heap of open vodka and wine bottles, plates of leftover food, a half-empty three-litre pickle jar, an ashtray overflowing cigarette butts and burnt matches. In the other, adjoining room, there was an untidy heap of all kinds of items.

"I apologize for the mess, but I expect you'll understand . . . Wait a moment . . ." said the wretched physicist and vanished into the kitchen.

Pavel Fyodorovich was unable to regain his composure. On the wall above the antiquated television set hung a large photograph. He moved closer to get a better look: it was Lenuța; she was young, smiling, standing next to the gate where they had once embraced. Unbelievable how many thoughts can rush into a man's mind in just a fraction of a second. He looked at the framed photograph in silence. Everything had a bitter taste, the taste of the irretrievable past.

His host returned from the kitchen with a carafe and a small plate with a few bits of bacon and slices of bread. From the table he took two dirty glasses, disturbing a few sluggish, sated flies, filled them to the brim, and handed one to Pavel Fyodorovich.

"May she rest in peace!" they both said simultaneously. The physicist knocked back his glass. Pavel Fyodorovich sipped the dubious liquid cautiously.

"How did she die?" he asked quickly, his temples throbbing.

"You don't know? In hospital . . . gynecological problems . . . when I came to get her, she was lying in a pool of blood . . ." the physicist murmured. His face tensed. He filled his glass once more and immediately knocked it back. Pavel Fyodorovich felt a burning pang in his heart.

Suddenly, the host lifted his bloodshot eyes and studied his guest.

"Who are you anyway? I don't think I know you . . ."

"Well, I don't know how to put it . . . I'm a colleague . . ." stammered Pavel Fyodorovich, unable to find his words.

"You're a teacher at Elena's school?"

"No, I meant that we were colleagues when we were students . . ." said Pavel Fyodorovich without conviction.

The physicist stared at him with bulging eyes. A suspicion was growing in him, and he rapidly became certain of it.

"You! You're the bastard who made her have to get an abortion so that she couldn't have children any more!" shouted the sturdy man, abruptly getting up.

Pavel Fyodorovich's heart quailed.

"You don't understand! I wanted to . . ." blurted the uninvited guest, taking a step back.

"Understand what, you bastard? That you killed my wife and you come here, now that she's dead, to laugh at me?" roared the physicist rushing at him so he could punch him.

Pavel Fyodorovich ran for the front door, but in the dark and consumed with terror, he was unable to open the lock. A fist like an artillery shell hit him in the back of the neck. Amid punches and curses, he was thrown out of the apartment like a bag of garbage. An old woman peeped from a half-open door in alarm, swearing about the hooligans and threatening to call the police. Pavel Fyodorovich limped down the stairs, filled with mingled shame, guilt, and objectless rage.

Lyusya had a bad feeling. She wasn't so blind as not to see that a deep change had come over her husband. He had become suddenly morose and distrait, he was off work and stayed at home in his office all day. True, sometimes he would sneak out, she didn't know where, and would come back later even more upset than before. But what alarmed Lyusya more than anything else was the fact that after twenty years of marriage Pavlusha spent the night in his office, leaving her in the bedroom alone. She was tormented once more by the thought she had struggled with all these years and which she had finally repressed: Pavlusha deserved to have a more beautiful wife.

"I've unfolded the bed, Pavlusha . . . I'm waiting for you . . ." she said in a trembling voice one evening, after having slept alone for a number of nights, but Pavel Fyodorovich shut himself up in his office, muttering angrily.

"He's sick of me," she thought, as she examined her wrinkled face in the mirror. Within the space of just a few days she had become fully aware of the uselessness of make-up and the perishability of the human body.

"Could this really be the end? Is the nothing that can be done?" she asked herself in despair. The most amazing thoughts flooded her mind: what if she was taken to hospital or by some miracle became pregnant to soften Pavlusha's heart, what if she had her fortune told in the coffee grounds . . .

Finally, she went to Panteleyevna; she asked the advice of her friend who had been through hell and high water. Evincing an air of superiority, the "expert" in marital problems explained to her colorfully and at great length that all men in their fifties go through a major depression and are tempted by adultery. The wife has only two options: to cut her losses and end the marriage or to swallow her bitterness, fight for her happiness, and defeat the charms of the mistress.

"I chose the second way, and I don't regret it," said Panteleyevna in a superior tone of voice.

Lyusya gasped.

"Do you think Pavel has . . . another woman?" she asked in a faint voice.

"What? It's obvious he has another woman. Why

would you think that your Pavel is any different from other men? I was as naïve as you once. I've long suspected he's sleeping with another woman, but I didn't want to break your heart . . ."

Lyusya felt the earth giving way beneath her. Never had she thought she might have a rival. The rest of the day, she fretted over the horrifying hypothesis. If there was a mistress, then the end was nigh. All they had built together in twenty years of marriage would go down the drain.

The days that followed, she started spying on him. She would tiptoe to the door of his office and listen for minutes at a time. She didn't learn anything much, only that her husband paced up and down, from wall to wall, with the regularity of a pendulum and that he kept having heated telephone discussions with somebody called Ion . . .

Since the crack of dawn, Lyusya had been up and about, busy in the kitchen. Marina went off to the market, taking an enormous bag with her. Garik was coming for lunch! By noon, the table in the dining room had been laid and was groaning with food. Filled with excitement, Lyusya took out a flowery dress and ceremoniously donned it. At the appointed hour, they persuaded Pavel Fyodorovich to come out of his office. But Garik did not make his appearance.

After half an hour of tense waiting—during which
Pavel Fyodorovich drummed his fingers on the
table—Marina telephoned the sister of her chosen
one and discovered that Garik was "on his way."

"Damn it to hell!" exclaimed Pavel Fyodorovich,
thinking how young people today lacked all sense of
responsibility.

Finally, after another half an hour of waiting, the
doorbell jangled. Marina rushed to open the door.
Lyusya flushed. Her daughter returned, radiant,
holding a freckled, long-haired young man by the
hand. He was wearing training shoes, scuffed jeans,
and a black t-shirt emblazoned with *Santana* in white
letters.

"Hello! I'm Garik. What's happening?" asked the
young man. He looked impassive and slightly bored.

Pavel Fyodorovich was all but thunderstruck, but
thinking that his daughter's happiness was all that
mattered, he managed to keep his cool.

"I am Pavel Fyodorovich, Marina's father, and this
is Lyusya Pavlovna, her mother. Sit down, young
man, and let's talk . . ." said the host, casting a sidelong glance at his wife. Lyusya seemed more delighted
even than her daughter and urged her potential son-
in-law to help himself to the repast.

"Stupid woman!" said Pavel Fyodorovich to himself.

He uncorked the champagne and poured the

frothing liquid into splendid crystal flutes. He then bid the others to clink glasses. The women sipped their champagne, while Garik and Pavel Fyodorovich knocked theirs back like fabled heroes.

"Marina tells us that you are studying History. What do you intend to do after you finish university?" asked Pavel Fyodorovich, getting straight to the point.

Garik replied only after masticating at leisure his mouthful of cold turkey.

"Well, I'm a bit sick of university, Pavel . . . Pavel . . . ah! Pavel Fyodorovich! It's damned tedious, and the teachers don't know what they're talking about. I'm thinking of jacking it all in and becoming an explorer. I want to go to the North Pole and see the polar bears!"

"You're joking, aren't you?" said Pavel Fyodorovich, raising his eyebrows.

"Of course I'm joking. The thought just came to me, like that. But wouldn't it be great to go to the North Pole? When you were young, didn't you ever want to do something like that?"

"No, I didn't . . ." said Pavel Fyodorovich, casting a meaningful glance at Lyusya, who was gazing up at the ceiling.

Garik poured himself more champagne, took a swig, and sank back in his chair with a belch. Marina was eating him up with her eyes. Lyusya hurried to replenish his plate. They were all silent for a few minutes.

"I am given to understand, young man, that you wish to ask my daughter's hand in marriage . . ." said Pavel Fyodorovich, sensing that the silence was growing awkward.

"Well, that's one way of putting it . . . Actually, we've agreed to get married," said Garik, with a sarcastic smile.

"Dad, you don't ask a woman's hand in marriage nowadays . . ." said Marina, backing up her boyfriend.

"That's as may be . . . But allow me to ask you, young man, how you intend to make a living? Where will the two of you live?" asked the host, raising his voice. The long-haired lad's impassive mien was starting to get on his nerves.

"Well, do we or don't we have parents? My *starik* will get us an apartment, don't you worry about that. We're not going to starve. I see you're not doing too bad yourselves. But in the event of an emergency, I can always go and work on the Siberian pipeline, swinging a sledgehammer!" said Garik in what would have seemed like a mocking tone had he not maintained the impassivity that so irked Pavel Fyodorovich.

"Pavlusha, Garik's father is the director of the Vibropribor factory!" Lyusya solemnly announced.

"So that's what the secret was! Not bad, but hardly

a big cheese . . ." Pavel Fyodorovich said to himself, feeling utterly confused. He then asked: "And does your father know the two of you are engaged?"

"Not yet, but it won't be a problem," said Garik, knocking back another glass of champagne.

"Yes, well . . . How is it that for you lot everything is as easy as pie?"

"You live a longer and more interesting life if you don't make complications for yourself," said Garik, producing a packet of Kent cigarettes from his pocket and asking for an ashtray.

"What the hell is going on with young people today? They wear Western clothes, listen to Western music, grow their hair long, they're adrift, anarchists, they don't have any ideals. And a many of them are the offspring of the bigwigs!" thought Pavel Fyodorovich.

He had the strange, vague sensation that the thoughts were not his, that they were something somebody had once told him and despite him having dismissed them, they had been stored in some corner of his mind, only to rise to the surface now. All of a sudden, he recalled the irritating, anxious veteran, what was his name? Polikarp Feofanovich!

Pavel Fyodorovich was sipping his coffee and solving a crossword puzzle when his secretary informed him that a veteran wished to speak to him.

"Why didn't you tell him that tomorrow is the day we receive people?" asked the deputy to the head of ideology, with a frown.

"He says he wants to tell you something important and besides . . . he's got so many medals!" said the secretary, looking guilty.

"Medals . . . Only he has medals?" growled Pavel Fyodorovich, closing his magazine. He then added, "Send him in . . ."

An old crock with a shiny bald head cautiously opened the door to the office, looked all around, cleared his throat, and greeted him.

"Take a seat, I'm listening . . ." said Pavel Fyodorovich, determined to end the discussion as quickly as possible.

The old codger seated himself, his medals jingling.

"My name is Pugovkin, Polikarp Feofanovich . . . I am a member of the Veterans Organisation, Ryshkanovka sector, I took part in the assault on the Reichstag and I worked in the Party's City Committee until ten years ago. Do you remember me?"

"No, I'm afraid I don't . . ." said Pavel Fyodorovich. A look of regret lingered on his face for a few moments.

"Yes, well . . . Actually, I came here to talk to you about something serious, very serious. The Party must take measures if things are not to deteriorate. If we close our eyes to it now, later we may no longer be able to do anything about it."

The veteran's face became harsh.

"Comrade veteran, I would ask you to be more specific . . ."

"That's what I was about to do. Can you imagine what happened to me not so long ago? A pioneer, who used to come to my house to tidy up, threw a rotten tomato at my head!"

Polikarp Feofanovich's voice was trembling.

"An unfortunate incident, comrade veteran, but I think you've got the wrong address. You say you know the pioneer in question. Why don't you talk to the head of his school or the local police? I'm in no doubt that they will take measures!" said Pavel Fyodorovich, annoyed at having to listen to the old crock's stupid problems.

"Yes, well . . . Let's say I go to the police and the pioneer is punished, but what are we to do with the others?" asked the veteran, his eyes boring into him.

"What others?" Pavel Fyodorovich couldn't make head nor tail of it.

"Imagine if the same thing happened to my friend Veniamin Nikanorovich, a man who defended Stalingrad! And not only to him!"

Pavel Fyodorovich shrugged. It wasn't the first time

he had wasted time with the veterans of the Soviet Army, but he had never had a discussion as absurd as this.

The old crock looked at him as if he were deserving of pity.

"You don't understand any of this, do you? When was the last time you left your office? I'm trying to explain to you that every day, hundreds, thousands of pioneers and Komsomol members are insulting veterans. Something serious is happening to the younger generation. They're impertinent, lazy, devoid of ideals. Don't you know that all the adolescents are listening to Western music? How many of them read Marx and Lenin in their free time? In my day, they'd put you in prison for behavior like that! Think about what will happen to our country when these addle-headed youngsters take over!"

Pavel Fyodorovich looked in wide-eyed amazement at the veteran, who was growing more and more agitated. It was by now quite obvious that his agitation was a result of mental derangement.

"Please calm yourself, comrade veteran. I get the impression that you are exaggerating. Have you ever visited the Artek to see what wonderful children we have there? Yes, there are deplorable cases, but we shouldn't generalize! And anyway, what do you want us to do? Punish every pioneer and Komsomol member? Absurd. I advise you to speak to the parents of that pioneer and I'm sure they will condemn his behavior. Good day, comrade veteran!" said Pavel Fyodorovich, no longer able to conceal his irritation.

"I didn't say that every pioneer and Komsomol member should be punished, but only that they are no longer educated properly. Education in school, in the family, in the pioneer and Komsomol organizations, everywhere, is shoddy! And the sons of the *nachalniki* act like boyars, they're westernized!"

"I'm going to have to ask you to leave, comrade veteran. I have a meeting," said Pavel Fyodorovich raising his voice, standing up.

Polikarp Feofanovich stared at him with desperate eyes and then softly said: "I know what you get up to at your meetings. You chatter away pointlessly instead of talking about what is destroying society from within. The time will come when you'll remember my words. But by then it will be too late . . ."

The tone in which he uttered these final words was one of profound weariness, disgust, and bitterness. He left the office, leaving the door open behind him. If he had not met Garik, Pavel Fyodorovich would not have now remembered the eccentric veteran.

Life cannot be crammed into the molds of logic. Life is full of absurd contradictions. Having been battered and kicked out of the apartment, Pavel Fyodorovich found himself standing in front of the same peeling door the very next day. They had a heated discussion, if, of course, you could call that torrent of harsh words, curses and accusations a discussion. The physicist yelled, glaring at him with bloodshot eyes. Pavel Fyodorovich took the entire blame on his shoulders and told the widower that he was just as devastated by Lenuța's death as he was. He had come to offer his condolences, to console him in his grief, but he could not accept to be beaten and humiliated. The physicist listened with clenched jaws and then started yelling again, accusing him of the death of the child and his wife. Finally, he calmed down, exhausted, overcome with despair.

After a moment's silence, the widower said in a faint voice: "You don't know the meaning of grief . . . You tell yourself that you have your whole life ahead of you and then one fine day there's nothing else you can do; it's too late. You don't know what it means to be alone and all of a sudden to feel life's emptiness. You have a family, I've lost everything . . ."

Pavel Fyodorovich abruptly realized that any explanation was useless, that whatever he said would only annoy him even more. He left straight away, but returned the next day. Together, they cleaned up the apartment and aired the rooms, ridding them of the smell of sweat, leftovers, dirty clothes. They went to the garbage cans with the leftover food, empty bottles, opened tin cans, under the watchful gaze of the old biddies with the overactive imaginations. Then they pensively drank the expensive brandy that Pavel Fyodorovich had brought.

Gradually, Pavel Fyodorovich's visits became a custom for both of them. They had become indispensable to each other, despite their mutual animosity. The invisible thread that bound them was Lenuța. Inexplicably, her face seemed to emerge from the void when they were together, only to fade away when they parted. And there was another thing: both of them were trying to find out more about Lenuța. One day, the physicist was struck by the astounding thought that he would never have married Lenuța if Pavel Fyodorovich had not been a coward. And the deputy to the official in charge of ideology then realized that he could not atone for his guilt before Lenuța unless the widower forgave him. Sometimes, Pavel Fyodorovich would go to the Academy of Sciences and give the physicist a lift home in the silver Volga. As a result, the standing and the salary of assistant Ion Puică were considerably augmented. Pavel Fyodorovich did not hesitate to provide him with material assistance whenever he was in difficulties. True, the physicist was not easily persuaded to accept Pavel Fyodorovich's help, and at first, he blew his top, feeling insulted. But in time he got used to it.

On the day when the two went to the Doina Cemetery and kept a long silence at Lenuța's grave, Pavel Fyodorovich invited the physicist to his daughter's wedding. For the past month he had been spending huge sums of money preparing one of the most lavish weddings Kishinev had ever seen. The important guests included the chairman of the Soviet of Ministers and the head of the republic's KGB. The stakes were very high and the father of the bride had personally seen to every detail, relegating the parents of the groom to the role of extras. He had spoken to every single waiter at the Intourist Hotel separately.

That evening, he sat in the armchair in his office, staring into space, thinking of how his life was depressingly monotonous. His daughter knocked on the door, entered, evincing embarrassment, and told him that she was no longer going to marry Garik. Pavel Fyodorovich was dumbstruck. He then leapt to his feet, yelling: "Are you out of your mind? What's got into you?"

"I now realize that Garik is a bounder, he doesn't love me, he flirts with other girls. I don't trust him. And besides, you yourself said that it's important I finish university . . ." whispered Marina, guiltily.

"You're insane! I've prepared everything, spent a lot

of money, sent out the invitations . . . Do you want to destroy me? You're getting married! Do you hear me!" Pavel Fyodorovich bawled, gasping for breath.

"I can't get married to a man I don't love . . ."

"You're getting married!" screamed Pavel Fyodorovich.

He saw black. His heart was fluttering like a bird in a cage. Suddenly, he felt an agonizing pain in his chest. He collapsed on the Persian rug. Terrified, Marina ran screaming from the office. Lyusya burst from the kitchen. After trying in vain to revive him, she rushed to the telephone and with trembling hand dialed 03.

He lived for a long time stretched out on a bed and all the while he did nothing but stare out of the window at the leaves of an old poplar. Once only did he look at the clock on the wall, whose hands seem to have frozen. He heard the voices of the other two patients, who played chess all day long. In the evening, after they grew tired of chess, the patients, one a pessimist, the other an optimist, were in the annoying habit of debating the meaning of life. The pessimist said that a man's existence is merely a series of days without any deeper meaning, while the optimist believed that *something* had to lie behind the everyday stage set. The argument stimulated Pavel Fyodorovich, although the doctors had warned him against any emotional disturbance. He wanted *something* to exist beyond the daily welter. In the ward, he had gained an awareness of his old age for the first time.

When Lyusya and Panteleyevna visited him for the first time after his heart attack, when he saw the alarm on the face of his wife, haggard with insomnia, Pavel Fyodorovich felt a pang in his heart. He felt a desire to take her hand in his, to reassure her, to tell her the thing he had never told her. He felt closer to her than he ever had before.

The School

IULIAN WANTED TO WATCH the hockey match between the Soviet Union and Czechoslovakia, but his father turned off the television and, looking him up and down, told him to learn the poem he had to recite at the school gala.

"What marks have you got this term?"

"A's and B's . . ."

"Get it into your head, you'll die of hunger if you don't study!"

Despite him having no idea what his son did at school, machinist Vladimir Vladimirovich constantly described to him the dim future that awaited truants and students who flunked the year. He worked at the Vibropribor factory from dawn to dusk for a wage of 100 to 120 rubles, he came home exhausted and testy, and so naturally he was unable to supervise his son. Even though he himself had read no more than two books in his whole life, he made Iulian read every day. The good part was that Vladimir Vladimirovich made no distinction between textbooks on Moldavian literature/history and science-fiction novels.

Deprived of the opportunity to watch the invincible Soviet hockey team teach the uppity Czechoslovaks some respect, Iulian took down from the shelf a volume by talented Soviet Moldavian poet Grigore Vieru and curled up in the armchair (bought on hire purchase, like all the other furniture in the apartment) in the other room. It was a poem by Grigore Vieru that he had to recite.

> *Mama pîine albă coace,*
> *Noi zburdăm voios.*
> *Pentru pace, pentru pace*
> *Mulțumim frumos.*

[Mama bakes white bread, / We gambol merrily. / For peace, for peace / We thank you kindly.]

It was the very poem that had caused him to make an embarrassment of himself in the last Moldavian Literature lesson. The humiliating situation now returned to his mind.

"Children, which of you can tell me whom the

lyric 'I' is thanking for peace?" asked Vera Georgievna, a warty, middle-aged teacher tortured by loneliness.

None of them could tell her. Vera Georgievna's eyes settled on the dreaming Iulian, who was admiring the wavy hair of the beautiful Lenuţa Timofte.

"He's thanking Mama . . ." blurted the boy, taken by surprise and saying the first thing that came into his head.

Vera Georgievna stared in surprise.

"What's that? We analyzed the Grigore Vieru poem only yesterday, you nitwit! Are you really stupid or are you just pretending?"

The boy with the long head turned red. He was flustered not only because of his blunder, but also because of the reproving look that Lenuţa with the wavy hair was giving him . . .

After learning the poem by heart, Iulian leafed through an atlas with dog-eared covers, printed in Moscow. It was more than a hobby. It was an all-consuming passion. Oblivious of everything else, he could examine the maps, and the political map in particular, for hours at a time. The Soviet Union was vast, but to Iulian it seemed small. The lad could not understand how there could be a South America, an Africa, an Australia outside the Soviet Union. How could there be an imperialist Germany after Hitler

had been annihilated? How could that pig of a tsar
have sold Alaska to the Americans? Iulian imagined
a Soviet Union that would stretch from Portugal to
San Francisco. He once asked his bewildered tutor at
school whether the USSR really was the most powerful
country in the world. Yes, it was, confirmed the tutor.
Then why hadn't all the imperialist countries been
destroyed? Because the Soviet Union was the bastion
of peace on earth. We are not conquerors, we merely
defend what is ours . . .

His mother woke him at the crack of dawn to recite
the Grigore Vieru poem. He ate his breakfast—cocoa
and fried eggs—crammed his textbooks into his bulging satchel and, urged on by the noisy ticking of the
clock, ran from the apartment. The walls of the stairs
were covered in Cyrillic graffiti: *Petya + Marina =
Lyobov'. Larisa, sosi khuy! Ala Pugacheva. Boney M.
Yulik durak! Valeria byk! Miru mir. Ne zabudu mat'
rodnuyu. Moya militsiya menya berezhet! Maldavanin
tuporylyy!*[22] On the football pitch in front of the housing block, veteran Aleksey Petrovich Lyulin—a real
Methuselah—was walking his bulldog, which had
just taken a shit in the penalty box. Not far from the
school, Iulian stopped to look at one of the few adver-

---

[22] Russian: "Petya + Marina = Love. Larisa, suck cock! Ala Pugacheva. Boney M. Iulian
is stupid! Valeria is a yokel. Peace to the world. I won't forget the motherland. My
police takes care of me! Stupid Moldavian."

tising hoardings of the Brezhnev era, which urged the people of Kishinev to fly Aeroflot. The advertisement was utterly pointless given that Aeroflot had no competitors, but it used to prompt Iulian to a daydream. He imagined flying with Chikalov above the boundless taiga. Sometimes, Grigore Vieru would be with them, and he would give them each a signed book of his poems. He passed some apartment buildings under construction, above which menacingly towered a crane that had once fallen over, killing a housewife on her way back from the market with laden shopping bags. The housewife had been his mother's best friend and it was very strange indeed that the fine, upstanding police had made no arrests.

The school assembly hall was packed: all-seeing inspectors from the Department of Education; teachers, those wise guides; parents, filled with emotion; veterans of the Soviet army, their medals jingling; and, naturally, large numbers of children (Octobrists, Pioneers, Komsomolists). Shuffling her feet, the obese cook from the canteen was there too; never had she dreamed of having so many customers. Above the stage hung a placard that read, *We Sing Peace and Friendship*, and in a corner of the hall a few curious children were examining a globe inscribed with the word *PEACE* in various languages.

Iulian was lucky: he was one of the performers.

Consequently, he was a pupil whose merits could not be doubted. A flushing girl pioneer rang a bell to announce that the fête had begun. A pupil whom Iulian envied for his public-speaking skills, passionately recited a poem by Liviu Deleanu:

> *Ridică-ți ochii dornici de minune,*
> *Copilule cu fruntea bucă . . . lată,*
> *Să vezi cît de frumoasă și bogată*
> *E necuprinsă noastră Uniune.*

[Lift your eyes eager for a miracle, / O, child with the curly brow,[23] / To see how beautiful and rich / Is our boundless Union.]

The audience applauded. It was an auspicious start; the teachers were pleased. A girl, who later, during Moldova's interminable post-communist transition period, was to become a prostitute in Albania, proclaimed with the utmost conviction: "The Union of Soviet Socialist Republics! It is my sweet land, it is yours, it is ours. It is the land where people genuinely forge a luminous future, it is the land of childhood happiness and dreams come true, it is the land of victories!"

Everything was going like clockwork. The children

---

[23] The reciter subversively inserts a pause into the word *bucălată* ("curly"), rendering it *bucă lată* ("broad buttock") — *Translator's note*

were animated; the inspectors had no reason to find fault with the teachers. Nevertheless, something unwonted occurred, an insignificant detail unworthy of attention and noticed only by Iulian. When the girl movingly declaimed, "it is the land of childhood happiness and dreams come true," somebody in the audience sniggered. A brief, barely noticeable snigger, but which conveyed disbelief. Or at least so it seemed to Iulian. Next up on stage was the son of a member of the nomenklatura, currently the head of a joint Moldavian-East German enterprise: "People of every profession—the peasant Chapayev, young doctor Shchors, Cossack Budyony, machinist Voroshilov"— with emotion, Iulian recalled that his father was a machinist—"agronomist Kotovski, and others—have joined the struggle against the country's internal and external enemies. And the self-sacrificing struggle of the Red Guards was not in vain: seizing for themselves the power of state, the working class defended their freedom and began to build a new world, a society without oppressors and without oppressed."

The audience applauded wildly. The history teacher cried, "Bravo!" A veteran was moved to shed a few tears. And once again Iulian detected a snigger, this time seemingly more defiant. It was now the turn of a boy in Iulian's class to speak. A shy lad, who was later to die in mysterious circumstances in Afghanistan, in 1987.

"22 June . . . The fascist thugs villainously invaded the Soviet Union. Thousands and thousands of shells rained down on Stalingrad, cities and villages wiped from the face of the earth, death camps, devastation and grief, looting, destruction and ash— this is what the war brought to our peaceful land. In defense of Peace and the sacred Homeland Gastelo and Kosmodemianskaya rose up, Matrosov and Soltys rose up, Koshevoy, Shevtsova and Glavan rose up, millions of sons and daughters of the Soviet people rose up."

In amazement, Iulian noticed that one of the war heroes had fallen asleep and was even snoring softly. But this in no way prevented the gala from continuing. A chubby girl, who today sells cucumbers and tomatoes in Kishinev's Central Market, gave a rousing speech: "Shoulder to shoulder, all the peoples of the country rose up to defend the Homeland. The friendship of the fraternal peoples struck like a huge hammer"[24] —here Iulian gave a start—"like a colossus at the breast of the enemy army. This was the greatest and most formidable weapon against the Nazis, who were finally vanquished. Victory belonged to those who have always wanted nothing but peace, to those who have befriended each other for all eternity, to all the peoples of our great country."

---

[24] The Romanian *ciocan*, also used a surname, Ciocan, means "hammer" — *Translator's note*

To the accompaniment of a mournful melody, a girl who now lives in Canada sternly declared that the Boris Glavan and his comrades in arms did not die only for their native soil. "They defended the Homeland, civilization and culture. They fought for Pushkin, Eminescu, Blok and Tchaikovsky." After the girl—who subsequent to the collapse of the USSR was to experience a sudden interest in the flora and fauna of Canada, and who was to telephone Iulian from Toronto in 2005 to complain that she could no longer stand the materialistic, insensitive Canadians—it was the turn of Andrei Rusu to speak, a decent lad whom Moldova's interminable transition was to oblige to take refuge in Romania, whose own transition seemed to be coming to an end: "Great, powerful, undefeatable is our Motherland! Her power resides in the fraternity and friendship of the fifteen sister-republics, of all the peoples of our land. She strides confidently into the future and my republic, since our boundless Homeland has more than a hundred peoples, my republic, which I love, assists her and makes her bloom! We are proud that we live in a country with millions of friends. The gold of Siberia, the wheat of Kazakhstan, the cotton of Uzbekistan, the tea of Georgia, the grapes of Moldavia are ours, they belong to us all. All the treasures of the Homeland are shared by the whole of the Soviet people. And the greatest treasure—Friendship—has taken deep and firm root for all eternity!"

Finally, it was Iulian's turn. Emotional, flushing, he began to declaim Grigore Vieru's poem. But barely had he recited a single verse when somebody at the back of the audience burst into noisy laughter. That somebody was splitting his sides, and given the solemnity of the occasion, his laughter could not have been more mocking, more insolent. Iulian froze, unable to speak. Everybody, including the veteran who but moments before had been sleeping uninterrupted, turned to look at the hooligan who had burst out laughing.

It was Satarovich, the terror of the school, a brutish, loudmouthed boy, who had robbed Iulian and punched him in the nose a number of times. The Satarovich legend had horrified some and fascinated others long before the "god" had made his appearance. It was rumored that he bashed those children who didn't willingly give him their kopecks. He smoked American Kent cigarettes, which were a rarity at the time. He told obscene jokes about Leonid Ilyich Brezhnev in the toilets, where the reek of bleach knocked out the weaker boys. He had chewing gum of every variety and "tickler" condoms he procured from sailors from Odessa, whose purpose only the initiated knew. His brother had been a sailor, but he had had to leave the merchant fleet because he had got divorced and was no longer a Party member. Satarovich sometimes pissed in the school yard heedless of who might see him—a fact subsequently confirmed by a number of astounded schoolgirls. His hands would be all over the girls in the dim cloakroom, from where the light bulbs constantly disappeared. He knew a rich widow of forty-five, who fed him and gave him money. He had a number of pairs of Lee and Wrangler jeans. He held the teachers in contempt . . .

The "god's" first public appearance was one cold, misty morning, when after gym class, the pupils were huddling inside the school's main entrance. Swearing like a trooper, Satarovich started throwing a basketball at the heads, backs, backsides of the terrified pupils. The girls were screaming at the top of their voices. But the "god" was unmoved. In the opinion of some, he was mentally feeble, but this was hardly likely. Iulian was at a loss to understand why this dangerous individual had not been expelled from the school. The fact that Satarovich went unpunished bewildered him; it was at odds with his sense of morality.

The "god's" laughter provoked first deathly silence, then a general murmuring. The all-knowing school director, Taisia Scorpan, nicknamed the Scorpion, rose to her feet and gesticulating emphatically, shouted: "Remove that impertinent lout!"

A few burly fathers, backed up by the physical

education teacher, rushed at Satarovich, and the indignant veteran who had been woken up roared, "Have you no shame, you hooligan!"

The "god" was bundled outside, calm was restored, but despite all that, Iulian was unable to continue. He felt the ground giving way beneath his feet. He knew that they were all waiting for him to speak, he could see Vera Georgievna waving her finger at him, he could hear the lines of the poem, which his fellow pupils were whispering to him, but he could not unclamp his jaws. Finally, the Scorpion grabbed him by the hand and hauled him off the stage. In the corridor, the scowling school director let go of his hand and dragged him the rest of the way by the ear. The visibly alarmed Vera Georgievna brought up the rear. He was taken to the staffroom where a bald inspector and none other than Satarovich were waiting. Both had downcast faces. Even the portrait of jovial children's writer Ion Creangă that hung on the wall looked downcast. Iulian's heart shrank to the size of a flea.

"You animal, how dare you mock the veterans who shed their blood for you!" screamed the Scorpion, giving full vent to her fury.

"It was him what made me laugh, *blya*'" the "god" promptly replied, glaring at Iulian and pointing his finger.

Satarovich's index finger was thick and had a large nail, beneath which the dirt was plainly visible. Iulian suddenly remembered the caricature of an imperialist he had seen in *Pravda*: a terrifying imperialist in a top hat, seated on a sack of dollars, was stretching his paws across the ocean to seize Europe. He had missiles for fingernails, but he was doomed to fail, because a worker in overalls was aiming his hammer (*ciocan*) at the grasping paws.

"What does that mean?"

"He asked me to make a noise when he had to read his poem 'cause he didn't learn it." Satarovich seemed imperturbable.

From his pockets poked some crumpled ocean maps.

"Is it true what this hooligan says?" asked the Scorpion, her eyes bulging in amazement.

Iulian kept his silence. He had to choose: to deny it and be beaten to a pulp by Satarovich or to confirm it and be punished by both parents and teachers. Overwhelmed by fear, he was unable to understand that silence was the worst option.

The bald inspector was drumming his fingers on the table.

"So, you're in cahoots," concluded the Scorpion. "You ought to hang your heads in shame, you hooligans! I'll make sure you get what's coming to you!"

"Taisia Borisovna, who are the boy's parents?" said the bald man, with a yawn.

"His father is a worker, and his mother, apparently, is a nursery-school teacher . . ."

"Hmm, well, that complicates things," concluded the inspector.

Iulian went home deep in thought. Rebellion gradually welled up in his soul, overcoming his fear. He couldn't understand why Satarovich had started to laugh when it was his turn to recite, rather than anybody else's turn. He couldn't understand why the Scorpion and the inspector had lumped him together with the "god." After all, he wasn't a hooligan, he didn't insult his fellow pupils, he studied hard . . .

How would Satarovich beat him up? Would he humiliate him in front of everybody, kicking him in the belly, or would he get him in the dark cloakroom?

And how would Lenuţa Timofte react when she found out he had been beaten up?

He burst into tears . . . He had once seen a moving film in which a Stakhanovite cow-milker had got engaged to a handsome, waggish collective farm worker, but who was something of an individualist. On the eve of the wedding, the cow-milker had met another collective farm worker, who wasn't handsome, but was more courageous, more honest, more respectful of the collective property. The cow-milker hesitated, agonized, but finally chose the ugly, sober, honest collective farm worker, as was fitting. Iulian realized that he was neither handsome, nor courageous, nor honest. He went home filled with an incurable sadness.

The Crane

ONE FINE SUNDAY, old-age pensioner Dochitza Barbalat was killed as she was walking home from the market with laden shopping bags, and news of the terrifying accident soon spread all over Kishinev, even before the local journalists were able to shake off their delightful weekend lethargy. A gigantic crane, towering over some apartment blocks under construction, had suddenly collapsed onto the yard of an adjacent building, squashing two trees and a Lada, scaring the wits out of some children at play, and crushing the hapless housewife to a pulp. In the blink of an eye, local residents and passers-by came running, and the yard was filled with the murmur of subdued voices. As a matter of course, somebody called an ambulance and the police, although in the circumstances there was not a lot either could do. A few of the eye-witnesses to the tragedy expressed their amazement at the precision with which the killer crane had struck its victim. One of them claimed that Dochitza Barbalat had seen the falling crane and would still have been alive had she not been hesitant to drop her heavy shopping bags and make a run for it. The parents comforted their terrified children, and in their minds, they thanked providence for its mercy. Meanwhile a number of agitated residents were asking each other what would have happened if the crane had fallen on top of their building.

Nicolae Barbalat was making compote and bottling pickles in the cramped, steam-filled kitchen. In his mind he was castigating his wife for her tardiness when a neighbour brought him the dumbfounding news. A three-litre pickling jar slipped from his hands and shattered on the floor. He rushed from the house and, guided by the shocked neighbour, ran to the yard, where a crowd of people were jostling each other. He elbowed his way through the throng and was confronted by a sight that made him freeze. He all but collapsed in horror. Beneath the crane, which stretched from one end of the yard to the other, blood was oozing from a mush of flesh and clothing. A few bell peppers, cucumbers, potatoes had tumbled from a shopping bag, left miraculously intact. His eyes bulging in terror, Nicolae Barbalat stepped toward the remains of his wife and realised that his entire life had now been turned upside down.

Dochitza Barbalat had been a meek, generous, gentle soul, and many people had been fond of her. "Why should something like that happen to somebody like her?" those who had known her said to themselves. That fate could be so cruel to a devoted wife and loving mother was inconceivable. After the funeral, Nicolae Barbalat festered at home for almost a month, prey to despair, thinking of Dochitza. From time to time, his son, his daughter-in-law, his friends telephoned, trying in vain to console him. He ate only sporadically; he ceased to shave or to brush his teeth. He lay on the bed, staring at the ceiling, where he saw the face of Dochitza, his inseparable, lifelong companion. His mind went back to when they were young, and he remembered how more than once he had lost his temper with her almost for no reason, how he had yelled at her merely because she had asked him to moderate his drinking. He pictured her on the day of their wedding, remembered how bashful and delicate she had been. He relived the excitement of the day when their only son had been born.

From time to time he would look at the death certificate, whereupon he would suffer a fit of nervous depression. His wife's death became more and more unbearable the more it dawned on him just how absurd the accident had been. How could a crane fall on top of somebody out of the blue? And not in some capitalist country where chaos and uncertainty reigned, but in the capital of Soviet Moldavia, the country where, as one writer of the people put it, "You overflow with confidence in the future, in what tomorrow will bring, in your own life and labour." The sudden death of his wife was a flagrant and agonising injustice, but it was also, above all else, *illogical*. True, people died untimely deaths in peacetime too, but it was one thing to die of a serious illness or a traffic accident, and quite another to be crushed by a falling crane. Why did the cursed crane have to fall on top of Dochitza in particular? Why couldn't it have fallen somewhere else?

Never in his long life had Nicolae Barbalat felt so powerless and so uncertain. It was impossible to change the past! He tossed and turned in bed night after night, eaten away by insomnia, thinking about the fragility of human life. To him, nothing seemed rational, or solid, or "protected by Law" any longer. Reality had suddenly become hostile and incomprehensible. One night, it occurred to him that he, his son, his grandchildren *each had their own crane*, and his heart began to thud violently. At the break of day, he telephoned his son and begged him not to let his grandchildren to walk anywhere near the construction sites. In the Ryshkanovka district there were numerous apartment blocks under construction; dozens of cranes towered menacingly, capable of cutting short innocent lives at any moment. He had become captive to this obsessive thought. His son assured him that he would keep a sharp lookout for cranes and begged him to eat and to get more fresh air. Rather than consenting to this, Nicolae Barbalat mumbled something unintelligible and hung up.

Who knows what would have become of the grieving pensioner if it had not occurred to him one morning that somebody had to be *guilty*. He leapt out of bed like a scalded cat. It was obvious that such an anomaly was explicable only if somebody were guilty: he had never heard of any other cranes collapsing in the Soviet Socialist Republic of Moldavia. He then recalled having read in *Vecherny Kishinev* articles criticising the *negligence* that resulted in damage and injuries in the workplace, and condemning failures to abide by construction regulations. The scales fell from his eyes in an instant. It was obvious that the crane had not collapsed out of the blue. The guilty party must be somebody on the construction site, perhaps the crane driver himself. Reality regained its coherence. His wife had died due to the negligence of some nameless, irresponsible villain. All of a sudden, he felt sick with hunger and weariness. He left the house and went to a food shop, walking shakily. The comely woman behind the counter stared in shock at the bearded, hollow-eyed apparition before her. Back at home, he ate his fill for the first time since Dochitza's death. He had to fortify himself. He harboured the conviction that the killer would be found and punished. And he would play an important part in that. He bathed, shaved, and phoned his workmate. They were doormen at the most expensive apartment block in Kishinev, working alternate shifts. The workmate was pleased that Nicolae Barbalat had managed to wrench himself from the claws of grief and told him that many of the bigwigs who lived in the building sent their condolences and had been looking forward to his return. After telling him that he would stay at home for a few more days until he was fully fit, Nicolae Barbalat got dressed, left his one-room apartment, and headed for the Ryshkanovka sector police station.

The police were up to their ears in work. Nicolae Barbalat had to wait an hour before a loutish-looking lieutenant finally invited him into his office.

"Out with it then, *papasha!*"

The loutish lieutenant had the air of somebody about to miss his train. Overcome with emotion,

Nicolae Barbalat told him that he was the husband
of the woman killed by a crane a month before. The
lieutenant knew that a crane had collapsed in his sector, he was sorry about the unusual occurrence, but
he could not understand why Nicolae Barbalat had
come to the police about it.

"I'm convinced that *negligence* on the part of somebody on the building site was behind it!" said Nicolae
Barbalat in a tremulous voice.

The old-age pensioner's supposition did not
impress the lieutenant. Quite the contrary. It plainly
irked him.

"Listen up, *papasha*, if it had been like you claim,
then we'd have called you the very next day. Or maybe
you've got some kind of evidence?" said the lieutenant, shifting restlessly on his chair.

Nicolae Barbalat was amazed. What, he was the
one meant to come up with evidence?

He told the lieutenant that he had doubts about
whether construction regulations were being obeyed
at the site. The lieutenant now lost his temper.

"You think we've got nothing better to do? What
do suggest? That we forget about bandits, burglars,
drunks, and murderers, and instead check to see
whether that crane was rusty? Or maybe you think
somebody pushed it over on purpose?" said the lieutenant, his voice rising and his eyes bulging.

Nicolae Barbalat was dumbfounded. Never would he have imagined that a guardian of public order could be such an ill-mannered yob. But he was not ready to give up. Barely holding his agitation in check, he demanded to speak to the policeman who had attended the scene of the accident. By now the lieutenant was foaming at the mouth with fury. Nevertheless, he made a telephone call and after an hour of torturous waiting for Nicolae Barbalat, a young man made his appearance: he told him that he had investigated the case and had come to the conclusion that the crane in question was not defective and that all the construction regulations had been obeyed.

"You're telling me that that damned crane collapsed out of the blue?" said the pensioner.

"Exactly! And instead of getting on with our work, we have to explain to you what would be glaringly obvious even to a halfwit!"

The loutish lieutenant waved his hand, dismissing Nicolae Barbalat, who left the office humiliated and seething with indignation.

WRITER OF THE PEOPLE, A. L.: *On the collective farms and in the factories, the management is particularly strict in abiding by the principle of granting citizens an audience and solving their complaints and requests without delay.*

In the ministries, the task of answering workers'
letters and petitions is systematically verified. We
have intelligent, warm-hearted leaders, but there
are rare instances of narrow-minded managers
guilty of abuses and despotic behaviour. You will
have read articles in the Soviet press in which
such anti-social actions are castigated. Measures
are taken and the solutions of such cases are made
public as a matter of duty.

But what about the other organs of state? Are
there only few people who enlist the help of the
labour unions? How many urgent and difficult
problems do the Party branches in every factory
and institution not solve? As soon as a citizen alerts
them, the police are ready to investigate public
order offences and to detain malefactors. The com-
rade judges deal with various conflicts and resolve
them in favour of the party who has justice on his
side. In this way, they defend human rights.

For the whole of the rest of the day, Nicolae Barbalat
thought about the lout who wore lieutenant's epaulettes. How could such a specimen work for the
police? Even if his supposition were incorrect, an
honest policeman ought at least to have taken it into
consideration. It was clear that the lout and his youth-
ful colleague had lied just to get rid of him. They

had covered up somebody's negligence because they couldn't care less, because they couldn't be bothered to move their arses for the sake of some old-age pensioner. But *Vecherny Kishinev* said that the authorities were combatting excessive bureaucracy and official indifference to ordinary people! Rebellion swelled in the widower's soul.

That evening he cooked himself some beans and then took from an album the nicest photograph of his wife. He gazed at it for a long while, wiping the tears from his eyes. The photograph had been taken many years previously: younger, smiling, slightly bewildered, Dochitza was wearing a low-cut white blouse and a skirt with red polka-dots, and in one hand she was holding an enormous shopping bag, from the top of which poked a leek and a French loaf. Nicolae Barbalat had borrowed the camera of a neighbour, a journalist, and had taken her by surprise as she was returning from the food shop. Later that night, without unfolding the sofa-bed, Nicolae Barbalat lay down with his wife's photograph under the goose-down pillow. He slept deeply for the first time in the last month, but early in the morning he was woken by a disturbing dream. He once more found himself in the office of the lout with the lieutenant's epaulettes, who was yelling at him: "Have you got any evidence?"

He knew what he had to do. After frying himself

some eggs—despondent at the thought that he didn't
have anybody to cook his food for him any more—he
rummaged determinedly through every drawer, found
his binoculars, and quickly went out. From afar he saw
that the killer crane had been replaced with another
that looked just as menacing. He prowled the perimeter of the building site until nightfall, keeping under
observation the machinery and hard-hatted constructors. Thanks to the binoculars, he was able to see the
constructors' eyes and divine their inner thoughts. He
did not notice anything suspicious, apart from the fact
that at one point a cement mixer fell to the ground
from a great height. It was a case of *negligence*, obviously, but it would not serve as conclusive evidence
for the police. Nor would it stand as evidence that
the workers on site swore using the foulest language,
although on the other hand, such coarseness went
hand in hand with negligence. The next day, Nicolae
Barbalat continued to prowl the perimeter of the construction site. The day after that, he was apprehended
while peering through a crack in the fence. A burly,
hard-hatted worker grabbed him by the collar and
yelled: "Caught you in the act, you old rascal! Trying
to pilfer the property of the people, were you? I'll show
you!"

A violent shove to the chest felled the old-age pensioner. The binoculars flew from his hand and the

lenses shattered as they hit a rock. He lay dazed for a while, his frightened eyes following the movement of the crane against the grey sky, before some passers-by finally helped him to his feet. He assured them that they didn't need to call an ambulance, and shakily made his way back to the home where nobody would be waiting for him.

Of all the bigwigs who resided in the apartment building by Pushkin Park, Pavel Fyodorovich Kavrig seemed the most congenial to doorman Nicolae Barbalat. He was less arrogant than the others and often exchanged a friendly word with the doorman. This is why, having lost all other hope, Nicolae Barbalat decided to ask his assistance. One morning, as Pavel Fyodorovich was leaving the building to go for a walk in the park, Nicolae Barbalat stopped him and blurted out the story of what had happened to him at the police station and the construction site.

"Pavel Fyodorovich, in the name of God, I beg you to help me!"

"How can I help you if you have no evidence?" asked the Party ideologue, looking at the doorman suspiciously.

"You can hardly believe that the damned crane collapsed out of the blue!" exclaimed Nicolae Barbalat, in the depths of despair.

"Hmm . . . Very well, I'll think about what might be done," muttered Pavel Fyodorovich. It was obvious from his face that he was none too pleased.

A week later, the doorman asked him whether he had been able to do anything about it. Pavel Fyodorovich slapped his brow: He had forgotten, damn it all to hell! Another week passed. The next time, Pavel Fyodorovich claimed to have been very busy. Nicolae Barbalat's final hope evaporated. He no longer believed the apparatchik would help him. Contempt for them all slowly took hold of him. They were all cut from the same cloth. That well-fed bigwig, that careerist out to get everything he could take, naturally didn't want to get into an argument with the police for the sake of a mere mortal like him. "Life is so unjust! It kills the people who are the worst off," thought the doorman.

One day, Nicolae Barbalat's son telephoned him and invited him to the repast they had prepared in remembrance of Dochitza's soul. Just as he was leaving work, he bumped into Pavel Fyodorovich. Haggard and upset, the ideologue told him that only now did he understand his pain and that he would demand the police clarify the circumstances in which Dochitza Barbalat had died. The doorman could not believe his ears. However, he did take note of the amazing transformation that had befallen the bigwig. What could have happened to him?

That evening, in his son's apartment, they performed the ritual in remembrance of Dochitza's soul. They poured out their grief and promised always to preserve her memory. The grandchildren could not believe their granny would not be buying them sweets and ice cream any more. At one point, Nicolae Barbalat turned his bloodshot eyes to the photograph on the wall. It showed the whole family, next to the statue of Stephen the Great by Pushkin Park: Nicolae Barbalat was wearing a grey suit jacket, his son and daughter-in-law were young and serene, the grandchildren were chubby and sulky, and Dochitza looked gentle, protective, holding a . . . what the hell! He stood up and went to the wall to get a better look. Standing slightly stooped, Dochitza was holding a huge shopping bag, stuffed with squashes. He suddenly remembered the nicest photograph of his wife, the one that immortalised her holding another shopping bag; he remembered that Dochitza had died while returning from the market with laden shopping bags . . .

In a fraction of a second the revelation dawned on him: All her life Dochitza had done nothing but lug shopping bags, cook his meals, put the laundry through the mangle. And a terrible suspicion seeped into his soul: He himself was guilty of his wife's death.

An Elucidation

"Why do you keep raking up the Soviet past? How much longer are you going to be its prisoners?" This is what an "emancipated" fellow writer barked at me one day. He's writing a novel about Moldova's interminable post-communist transition period. He was annoyed and wondered whether I was somehow a continuer of socialist realism. I was puzzled by this older writer, who had once won the Prize of the Union of Romanian Writers. Not because he couldn't understand that I had no truck whatsoever with socialist realism, but because the Soviet reality that so repulsed him had caused the chaos of the transition he was describing. I realize that this intransigent fellow writer has "liberated" himself from the tyranny of the Soviet past once and for all. But my situation is more complicated. As for me, I just can't exorcise my own ghosts. That's why I study them, barely suppressing my unease, I allow them to speak as I write. I have the feeling that only in this way can the past be borne and understood.

It was there in the Soviet past that the first and most important sequence of my life unfolded: childhood. If I had not been a Soviet child, I perhaps might have written only about the transition or I would have invented narrative worlds. I "rake up" the Soviet past because my present bears the deep scar of that past. And another thing: If we discount mounds of socialist-realist and pro-Soviet books, then we may easily conclude that the Soviet reality is still virgin soil, an almost unknown world. Solzhenitsyn and others wrote at great length about a terrifying, Orwellian Soviet reality: internal exile and the Gulag. Less is known about the *everyday*, the semblance of prosperity and peace, the grotesque, absurd, often comical façade of that tragedy, a façade which, assiduously polished by the socialist realists, became alluring even to some Westerners. I am inclined to think that the narrator of *Humboldt's Gift* is not far from the truth when he says that New York dreamed of breaking away from North America and joining the Soviet Union. It would be interesting to see a New York ruled by the "father of the nations." Would Stalin succumb to bourgeois ways or would New York be turned into a communist Berlin?

Well, you might tell me, and you would be perfectly right, that the novels of Viktor Erofeyev, Vladimir Sorokin, Ludmila Ulitskaya and other well-known post-Soviet novelists describe everyday life in the Soviet Union in great detail. It's true, except that there was not a single Soviet everyday, the same for a Russian, a Moldavian, a Tungus, for the centre and the periphery, for every social stratum. The aforementioned novelists write, as is only natural, about the everyday that they know, about their own dramas. They refuse and are unable to see the Soviet everyday through the eyes of an Uzbek or to feel what somebody at the Latin periphery of the Empire felt. This is why there is a risk of a limited, distorted perception of everyday life in the Soviet Union, so long as you yourself do not confess what you experienced. In the novels of Ludmila Ulitskaya, for example, you discover only that Moldovans "with drooping moustaches" deposit mounds of garbage on the coast of the Black Sea. I've no idea whether that is true. But let's not forget that we are dealing with a fiction in which reality is merely a starting point. I don't know whether Ulitskaya has any idea that the coast in question once belonged to Romania. What interests me is something else: can you form an opinion about the everyday life of Moldovans in the Soviet Union based only on this one detail? Hardly likely. I am not accusing the

Russian novelist of anything and I realize that what
is at stake is something else entirely. What I want to
say is only that nobody knows better than yourself
what you have experienced and nobody can tell the
story in your place.

Therefore, I return to a childhood that emanates a
vast sadness, during which the long hours were dragged
out over endless days, and the other side of the comical
and grotesque was the tragic. I cling to my memory
with an acute sense of unease. A childhood in a closed
world, which stifled any alternative in the cradle,
might have provoked revolt or disgust in me now,
but what I feel as I descend into the past is merely
unease. A consuming unease, it is true. What is for
sure is that I hold on to the memories without hatred,
without any thirst for revenge, without feeling sorry
for myself. If you feel sorry for yourself, if you weep
and yell, you risk shattering the drama of the situation and frightening the reader. The ideal thing would
be to give up your own subjectivity and employ the
narrative technique of the film camera or, at the very
least, to employ multiple viewpoints, to show that the
same thing can be simultaneously comic and tragic,
absurd and amusing, depending on the position from
which you look at it.

In fact, it is sufficient only to capture the tragic
and dissolve it in irony; by no means should you be

over-emphatic. Even if your soul aches, when you write you should think about how for most people your problems are *secondary*, unimportant, that you cannot be credible and authentic if you are self-pitying. Pure tragedy is no longer so obvious in a world in which horror is everywhere and enters your house along with the morning news bulletin. This is why, in order to throw it into relief, what is needed is Shklovsky's *estrangement*, that is, you have to show its amusing, bizarre, absurd side. And if it seems to you that a tragic event does not have such a hidden side, then conjoin it with some amusing or bizarre event. In that way, you will bring it to light.

The Spidola

NOTHING FORETOLD THE CATASTROPHE in the summer of 1982. As usual, his father got up before the break of day and still half-asleep went to the factory, his mother did the chores in their tiny kitchen or knitted mohair sweaters, and the tireless Aunt Sanya scoured the parks for bottles all day long. Iulian was on holiday. He read novels by Kurt Vonnegut and the Strugatsky brothers, sweating abundantly in the apartment, which baked in the unforgiving sun. The torrid weather would have been more easily borne at the seaside, but that summer they didn't go to Koblevo because they'd bought a sideboard on hire purchase. Nothing foretold the catastrophe before the day when his father brought home the Spidola: a superb, brand new transistor radio, probably the best available at the time, which the factory management had given

him for "twenty years of heroism in labor." A highly
expensive luxury item, which the worker, obsessed
with acquiring necessities, would not have ventured
to buy. But the factory had given him it for his devo-
tion, exceeding his expectations and making him conclude that somebody highly placed appreciated his
career and was thinking of him. In all likelihood, the
gift would have been something even more expensive
if Vladimir Vladimirovich had been a Communist.
But Olga Leonovna, who could never forget that at
the funeral of her father a communist had prevented
the priest from officiating the service, persuaded him,
after a heated discussion, to give up all thoughts of
becoming a Party member.

That the Spidola was radically different from the
vacuum-tube television set was something that the
boy with the long head understood from the very first
evening. All you had to do was turn the two knobs
and you entered another dimension. The world suddenly became vast, colorful, mysterious. For the first
time ever, the professional, optimistic voices of the
Soviet singers and presenters now had competitors:
a mind-boggling mixture of melodies, accents, and
unfamiliar languages. For minutes at a time, Iulian
could listen enthralled to a strident or hysterical voice
without understanding a single word. Who were
these people? Where did they live? What did they

do? He was hugely enamored of the pop music that the Spidola now made accessible.

The tide of foreign voices ebbed and even vanished during the day, pouring back only toward evening. During the day, the Spidola belonged to his mother and Sanya, who listened to the folk music broadcast by Radio Jassy. The Romanians' music sounded exactly like the Moldavians' music, because a part of Stephen the Great's Moldavia had been occupied by Romania. Sometimes, Iulian thought that the Soviet Union ought to liberate Romania's Moldavians. Which is to say, Romania, as a friendly socialist country, ought to give back the territory to Moldavia. It was unknown why Romania was in no hurry to do so. In the evening, his father would come home and, after eating his dinner, he would listen to the radio with the volume turned down low for a few minutes and then turn it off and go to bed, exhausted. It was then that the transistor was at Iulian's disposal He would go to his room and for hours at a time he would sit cross-legged on the fold-out bed, turning the knobs. Alongside, worn out by her explorations of the city's parks, Aunt Sanya muttered in her sleep. (She was to die five years later, and Iulian Ciocan, conscripted into the army as a telegraphist, was unable to go to his aunt's funeral. He was to sob silently, like an old man, behind a storeroom on the military base, so that nobody would see him.) At eleven o'clock, his mother entered the room, amazed that the light was still on. But the boy with the long head continued to listen to the radio in the dark. The spell was even stronger in the darkness slashed at intervals by the headlights of passing cars.

One evening, he came upon an unknown station at a place on the dial that had previously stabbed his eardrums with a piercing whistle. At first, he thought a Soviet presenter was talking. But within seconds he pricked up his ears. The man, who spoke perfect Russian, said that in order to halt Soviet expansion, the American president had ordered the building of neutron bombs. The first warheads had already been mounted, and within hours they would arrive in Western Europe. Iulian was stunned. He quickly turned off the radio. He had never before heard the voice of the enemy. Although his history teacher had warned him countless times that nowadays they were trying to blacken the name of socialism, without military intervention, without economic blockades, without setting fascist Germany against the Soviet Union, without diplomatic boycotts, the voice of the enemy had seemed distant and harmless to Iulian. But now that voice had impertinently entered his own home. His amazement slowly turned to indignation. That man deserved a punch in the mouth, in the spirit of poet Nicolai Costenco:

Vrăjmașul lacom și cu ochi fierbinți,
de-o vrea să muște, o să-i dăm la dinți!

[Greedy foe with burning eyes, / if he tries to
bite, we'll punch him in the teeth!]

But how could you punch a capitalist who was hundreds of kilometres away? The history teacher had told
them that the enemy voices had been ordered to spare
no effort in the "human" mission to defend human
rights in the socialist countries. Was it a paradox? A
ridiculous mistake? How could you defend the working class from the working class? Tractor drivers from
tractor drivers? And who was supposed to defend
them? Wolves in sheep's clothing are still wolves.
"After all, the voices of these 'defenders'," stressed the
history teacher, "are firmly rooted in the past, when
the 'defenders of human rights' collaborated with the
fascists during the war, and today their voices sound
tinny and in their throats seethes hatred for everything that has been won through honest labor in the
countries from which they fled, having committed
their crimes there."

There were two things and that both confused him
and made him uneasy: the calm and even pleasant voice
of the capitalists' presenter and the existence of the neutron bomb. He often talked about the neutron bomb

with Larik and the other boys at school. Naturally, the Soviet Union had its own weapons, but the mere fact that the imperialists possessed a super-bomb, an unmatched weapon of mass destruction, was terrifying. What would happen if some capitalist madman started a war? The Soviet Union would promptly strike back, no doubt about that, but how many people would survive and would our country prevail? That was the nub of the matter, according to Larik. It was possible for the entire planet to be destroyed. And what could be done about it? Almost nothing. If the Soviet Union were to attack first, the outcome would still be the same, believed Larik. Damn the capitalists! That evening, Iulian didn't turn on the radio. For a long while, he watched the beams of the car headlights sweeping across the ceiling and because of his unease he had great difficulty falling asleep.

For the next few evenings he avoided that venomous radio station. A Soviet schoolboy ought not to listen to the ravings of the enemy. Nevertheless, he was eaten away by curiosity. He wondered whether there might be justification for his interest. He told himself he was a convinced pioneer and consequently could not be influenced by capitalist demagogy. He wanted to listen to that radio station only in order to see how far the villainy of the capitalists could go. But on the evening when he searched for the station, he

was met once more by the piercing whistle. The capitalist station had vanished. He found it again a week
later, on an evening when he ate macaroni cheese. He
was turning the dials, thinking of Lenuța Timofte, a
girl in his class. He was in love with her and was afraid
that she was unaware of the passion that tormented
him. But he was also afraid that war might break out
before he could reveal his love to her. This time, the
man with the calm, pleasant voice was talking to two
other men about nothing less than the health of
Leonid Brezhnev! They said that the Soviet leader was
suffering from a serious illness, that the doctors had
tried in vain to prolong his life, and they wondered
whether Kremlin policy would change after the death
of the Secretary General of the Communist Party of
the Soviet Union. The incredible thing was that the
three did not seem very happy about the impending
death of their enemy. On the contrary, they seemed
to be sorry about the sufferings of an ailing old man.
Once more, Iulian was left perplexed. It was true that
there were a lot of jokes about Leonid Ilyich being
feeble old crock, but Iulian had never imagined that
the Secretary General could die. Jokes were jokes,
whereas the capitalists were talking with the utmost
seriousness about the imminent demise of Leonid
Ilyich. How dare they say that! They were probably
trying to demoralize the Soviet people, although if

Iulian thought about it, the Secretary General did look a bit tired.

COMRADE L.I. BREZHNEV: *In this region, where only one in ten knew how to sign their names, there is now a detachment of three hundred thousand scientists, engineers, agronomists, teachers, doctors, writers, and artists. One might say that in the history of the Moldavian people there has never been a period in which the national culture has flourished so intensely and multilaterally as it does now, in close interaction with the spiritual creation of all the fraternal peoples of our country.*

In the morning, after he ate his cheese omelet and fried potatoes, he asked his mother whether Brezhnev was going to die. Olga Leonovna raised her eyebrows.

"Well, he's old. He could die at any time. Haven't you seen that he can't read out his reports any more?"

His mother gave a brief laugh, but straightaway grew serious once more.

"That's not true! He reads them, but . . . a bit more slowly than before," retorted Iulian, surprised that his mother's view coincided with that of the voice of the enemy.

His mother shrugged.

"But what will happen if . . . if he dies?"

"Nothing will happen. They'll replace him with somebody else, the way he himself replaced Khrushchev."

"Will everything be the same as it is now?"

"Of course it will. But what's got into you that you're asking about Brezhnev?"

"I never thought he could die . . ."

"Everybody dies, so don't be too upset about it . . ."

The whole summer, the voice of the enemy talked about the death of Brezhnev. If it was really true that Brezhnev could die, why weren't the Soviet newsreaders talking about it? In September, after he returned to school, none of the teachers seemed worried about the possibility that the Secretary General might die. On 7 November, the whole family sat down in front of the ancient television set to watch the October Revolution Day celebrations in Moscow. Every year, Iulian looked forward to the military parade with great excitement. No army in the world was more powerful than the Red Army! That's why the capitalists invented the neutron bomb. They were afraid of a fair fight. But that cold grey November day, Iulian wanted most of all to convince himself that the Secretary General was in good health, that the predictions made by the venomous voices were bare-faced lies. He wanted the imperialists to see a powerful leader and to burst with envy. He waited with a pang of the heart for Brezhnev to appear on the viewing stand. And there he was at last, raising his feeble hand in a salute before letting it fall back down, limply. His mother's reaction was prompt: "His days are numbered . . ."

Iulian felt something crumble inside him.

Three days later everything came to a head; time abruptly came out of hibernation. All the newspapers announced the sudden death of comrade Leonid Ilyich Brezhnev, all the radio stations broadcast depressing music, all the teachers at school dressed in black and gave mournful speeches to their not very sad pupils. His mother went to her nursery school dressed in white and wearing bright red lipstick, much to the shock of the school's director and the representative of the Ministry of Education.

Iulian pictured over and over again the terrible image of the heavy coffin being lowered into the grave, thinking that an annihilating war could begin at any moment.